HAMMETT UNWRITTEN

a novel

Owen Fitzstephen

Notes and Afterword
by Gordon McAlpine

SEVENTH
STREET
BOOKS™

59 John Glenn Drive
Amherst, New York 14228-2119

Published 2013 by Seventh Street Books, an imprint of Prometheus Books

Cover image ©2012 Shutterstock
Cover design by Nicole Sommer-Lecht

Inquiries should be addressed to
Seventh Street Books
59 John Glenn Drive
Amherst, New York 14228–2119
VOICE: 716–691–0133
FAX: 716–691–0137
WWW.PROMETHEUSBOOKS.COM
17 16 15 14 13   5 4 3 2 1

Library of Congress Cataloging-in-Publication Data

Fitzstephen, Owen.
    Hammett Unwritten : A novel / by Owen Fitzstephen ; Notes and Afterword by Gordon McAlpine.
        pages cm
    ISBN 978–1–61614–714–3 (pbk.)
    ISBN 978–1–61614–715–0 (ebook)
    1. Hammett, Dashiell, 1894–1961—Fiction. I. McAlpine, Gordon. II. Title

PS3606.I889H36   2013
813'.6dc23

2012040717

Printed in the United States of America

To the black bird

"All of my characters are real.
They are based directly on people I knew, or came across."

—Dashiell Hammett

New York Evening Journal, 1934

San Francisco Examiner
April 2, 1922

MURDER OF SEA CAPTAIN LINKED TO BLACK FALCON AFFAIR

San Francisco, CA—SF Police confirm a link between last week's murder of Louis Doyle (44), master of the thirty-ton freighter *La Palacio*, and the recent criminal activity known as the Black Falcon Affair. "Captain Doyle was shot by Cletus Gaspereaux (46), aka 'the Big Man,' in an unsuccessful attempt to take from the captain's possession the statuette known as the Black Falcon," said Tom Paulson of the San Francisco Police Department. "Doyle had transported the *objet d'art* aboard his ship from Hong Kong in partnership with Moira O'Shea (24) and Emil Madrid (38), both of whom were later arrested as co-conspirators in his murder. Mr. Gaspereaux was slain in a shootout with SFPD."

Doyle's shooting occurred on the night of March 26 at Miss O'Shea's apartment on the one thousand block of California Street. A man of great physical size and strength, Captain Doyle managed, despite his wounds, to escape his assailants and make his way to the Pinkerton Detective Agency, where he died after delivering the Black Falcon into the hands of private operative Samuel Dashiell Hammett (26), who had been investigating the case. Subsequently, Mr. Hammett led authorities to the guilty parties.

"The irony of the whole affair," Paulson said, "is that the Black Falcon is a worthless counterfeit. It's nothing more than a crudely carved, black rock. Nonetheless, the results of its violent pursuit, which continue to reveal themselves to our shocked, law-abiding city, are sadly authentic."

NEW YEAR'S EVE, 1959

D ashiell Hammett stood alone on a residential, moonlit lane on the north shore of Long Island, one overcoat pocket heavy with a .38 and the other pocket weighted by housebreaking tools—files, picks, skeleton keys—that he hadn't used since his private investigator days in San Francisco almost forty years before. In the afternoon, he'd rummaged through his closet to find the tools; in the process, he'd come across typed notes for his own obituary that a journalist friend had lifted from a desk at the *New York Times* a few years back and presented to Hammett to commemorate his then-recent, unexpected recovery from a heart attack. Tonight, Hammett had slipped the obit into his coat pocket to remind himself that its publication was never abandoned, only postponed, and that if his actions on this New Year's Eve seemed desperate it was because his was now a desperate situation. On the drive from the city, in the dim glow of traffic lights, he'd read the typed page; with each reading, he felt more estranged from the man the obit attempted to describe:

> Writer Samuel Dashiell Hammett, the tall, slender master of "hard-boiled" detective fiction, died yesterday of heart failure at Lennox Hill Hospital in New York City. (Confirm details with hospital, incl. exact time of death and family members in attendance etc.) Born in 1894 in Saint Mary's County, Maryland, Mr. Hammett published over eighty short stories and five novels, "Red Harvest" (1929), "The Dain Curse" (1929), "The Maltese Falcon" (1930), "The Glass Key" (1931), and "The Thin Man" (1934). His best work transcended genre and was com-

pared to Hemingway; this newspaper described his prose style as "lean, driving, hard."

Mr. Hammett left high school at age fourteen and worked numerous odd jobs. At age twenty-one he became an "operative" with the Pinkerton National Detective Agency, working for seven years as a private investigator (primarily in San Francisco) before embarking full time on his writing career.

Married to Josephine Dolan in 1922, Mr. Hammett fathered two daughters. Later divorced, he began a long romantic relationship with Lillian Hellman, assisting in her development as one of America's premier playwrights. During World War II he served (at age forty-eight) in the Aleutians. In 1951, at the height of the McCarthy hearings, Hammett refused to give incriminating information about alleged communist members of a group he chaired, the Civil Rights Congress of New York, and was sentenced to federal prison, where he served five months. Upon his release, at age fifty-seven, he encountered worsening health and financial problems. Mr. Hammett never published another novel after 1934. (Why not? Must ask around the newsroom . . .)

Why not indeed?

It was seven years now since the unfinished obit and twenty-seven years since Hammett's last book; he'd never intended to stop writing but had seemed to just dry up, which was why he was standing now in this quiet, upscale neighborhood, resolved not to leave without acquiring a particular *objet d'art*, a talisman, that he'd come to believe had figured in all his old triumphs.

Crazy, of course. Hardly hard-boiled.

But it was life, not fiction.

Lily was in the city, attending a party. Hammett had claimed to be too sick to join her. Naturally, she didn't fuss. Since his recent diagnosis—which she had told him was a mere pulmonary infection but that he knew from a surreptitious glance at the doctor's files was a tumor for which the prognosis was his death in six to eight months— she hadn't fussed about much. She was patient these days, almost easy-going. At his worst times, he suspected her new gentleness was offered less for his comfort and more to alleviate whatever contradictory emotions she would otherwise feel upon his death. She knew as well as anyone that a strong final scene could save an otherwise uneven play. At his best times, however, he dismissed such cynicism and allowed her to dote on him. Tonight was neither among his best nor worst times. He had merely observed her as she pretended to be disappointed when he begged off the party. He didn't blame her. She deserved a good time. She'd always deserved more than he could give, he thought.

"But what will you do with your New Year's Eve, Dash?" she had asked, flitting distractedly about his room in her apartment, straightening his scattered books and notepads, which he would have to sort through later to reorganize into his slipshod system.

"Lily, I don't give a damn what date it is on the calendar."

"But one mustn't just ignore New Year's."

"Why not?"

"Because it tempts fate."

A cruel but irresistible comment entered his mind. "There's always next year, Lily."

She stopped straightening the room but said nothing.

"I'm sure I'll be feeling much better by then," he continued.

"Yes, Dash. I'm sure you will."

She was a better playwright than she was an actress, he thought.

"Still, I hate to think of you sitting alone by the radio at the stroke of midnight listening to Guy Lombardo," she said, turning to a pile of *Time* magazines that she began sorting into chronological order on an otherwise disordered shelf.

"What have you got against Guy Lombardo, Lily? Or is it his Royal Canadian Mounties you object to?"

"I can't bear the image that conjures in my mind."

"Grown men in Mounties uniforms playing trombones?"

"No, you in pajamas listening to the radio while outside all of Manhattan . . ."

"Don't worry, that won't happen," he interrupted. "No radio. I'll watch Guy Lombardo on the TV. And I'll put on a tie."

"I can't leave you alone tonight."

"Don't be silly. Go."

"Are you sure?"

"I wouldn't have it any other way."

Lily acquiesced.

Hammett knew she would, which is why he had chosen this evening to come to King's Point.

Now he stood at the property line of 416 Cavanaugh Lane.

The place was right out of *Town & Country*.

Who'd imagine that the statuette known as the Black Falcon, whose true story had inspired the iconic object in his novel *The Maltese Falcon* (as well as the spilling of much real blood) would be found in so quiet and respectable a burg? The house was large and well-proportioned— no boxy mansion. The grounds were well-tended and on a frosty field at the side of the property he recognized a large metal sculpture—a Calder, all angles and curves and spatial contradictions. The house was dark but for a carriage lamp that burned near the garage, a porch light that illuminated a large, well-made front door (upon which hung a Christmas wreath), and a flickering blue glow that slipped from behind the drawn blinds of an upstairs room. A television. Hammett expected the house to be unoccupied, having learned that the widow Paxton had accepted an invitation to a party in Manhattan. Perhaps the house-keeper was home. The detective in Hammett didn't like surprises. He knew well enough to respect their danger—particularly as he wasn't here tonight in the role of detective but as something more akin to a burglar.

He considered going back to the car.

But time was short.

Waiting for the perfect moment was no option when all that remained of his life could be measured in months. It had never been a good option. Recently, he told a newspaperman that the cause of his decades-long writer's block was that as a young man he'd written the last third of a novel in a single, thirty-hour sitting and that since then he'd believed he could do it again if circumstances lined up just right. He'd waited, but circumstances never lined up. Of course, now he attributed his writer's block to something too esoteric to explain to any journalist—unless, that is, the ghost of H. P. Lovecraft or E. A. Poe took up writing the literary column for one or another cosmopolitan rag, which he didn't consider likely even in a universe as strange as this one. No matter. A pagan holiday like New Year's Eve was the right time to make his play for the Falcon, he believed, regardless of who might be in the house. He kept to the shadows as he moved through the front gate and up the walk.

He would be stealthy.

And if discovered, he would be clever with words.

And if disbelieved, he would be violent.

He was still Samuel Dashiell Hammett, for God's sake—or at least, a close approximation.

Nearing the porch, he heard the television. The night was freezing and he'd expected the house to be sealed tight. Still, he'd not be climbing through any open windows. He was sixty-five years old and his weight had dropped to one hundred and twenty pounds. He had no illusions about being a Cary Grant–type cat burglar (and even Cary Grant was too old to be traipsing on the rooftops of Monte Carlo, he thought). He stepped onto the porch, which he hoped would not creak beneath him. If he could hear the television playing inside, then whoever was watching it might hear him out here. An old movie; he couldn't distinguish dialogue but only the strings and rhythms of a thick musical score. He moved to the front door, reaching for the knob before stopping cold. From here, he made out the dialogue from the movie.

It wasn't just any movie.

It was Bogart in the role of Sam Spade talking to Sydney Greenstreet as Kasper Gutman: "Now let's talk about the black bird," Bogart said.

Hammett froze.

"Mr. Spade, have you any conception of how much money can be got for that black bird?" Greenstreet said, his voice oozing decadence. The words were Hammett's, taken by Huston directly from the book. Hammett didn't have to see the TV to know that the scene was set in Gutman's hotel suite. He'd visited the studio on the day they shot it— almost twenty years ago now. Afterward he'd gone drinking at a dive on Sunset Boulevard with Bogart and Peter Lorre. He looked around. Was this a setup? Or some kind of joke? No one knew he was coming. Not even Lily. Still, Hammett didn't trust coincidence. Then again, maybe it wasn't such a long shot—Channel 9 in New York ran *The Maltese Falcon* so often on their *Million Dollar Movie* that Hammett sometimes joked he should own an interest in the TV station by now.

"You mean you don't know what that bird is?" Greenstreet continued.

"Oh, I know what it's supposed to look like," Bogart said. "And I know the value in human life you people put on it."

A snap and the blue light at the window died.

The voices stopped.

Hammett considered: the inhabitant of the Paxton residence was either going to bed now or had heard something suspicious and was dialing the police. He thought going to bed the more likely possibility. Nonetheless, he couldn't help considering what prison sentence would accompany a breaking-and-entering conviction in light of his previous record. Two years? Five? For a man with lung cancer, either was a life sentence. The prospect of dying behind bars was a humiliation that only the most sublime loot could tempt him to risk.

He took a deep breath, then removed his tools and knelt before the door.

Was the ease with which he picked the lock an auspicious sign?

He stood, opened the door, stepped inside, closed the door behind him, and removed a penlight from his pocket. Before he could turn it on, however, someone switched on a lamp, illuminating the entry. Hammett froze. From behind him, the direction of the staircase—a woman's voice:

"Who are you?"

He recognized the voice, though it had been decades since he'd last heard it.

"Get out," she continued. "Or I'll call the police."

Already, everything was going wrong. But perhaps there was enough left of Sam Hammett, private detective, to salvage the moment. Then he heard Lillian's voice in his head, asking *What on earth were you thinking by breaking-and-entering, you foolish old man*? He had hoped he wouldn't have to display the .38. Now he had no choice but to show the damn thing, which he slipped out of the inside pocket of his coat as he slowly turned around.

NEW YORK CITY, 1933

H ammett was alone when he heard knocking at the door of the suite he and Lily shared at the Hotel Pierre on Fifth Avenue. He was reclined on a couch, leafing through the galleys of his new novel, *The Thin Man,* which was scheduled for publication in just a few months. It would be his fifth novel in six years. Quite productive—particularly considering all the drinking and parties. He thought the new book well-constructed, clever, and witty (perhaps not the most refined qualities one can ascribe to a book, but hard-won nonetheless). Additionally, he thought its characters accurately reflected the cynical, self-absorbed whirl of New York society, and he particularly liked the relationship of the protagonists, whose hard-drinking, wisecracking ways were based on the lifestyle he and Lillian Hellman had shared almost from the first day they met, three and a half years before.

There was more knocking at the door.

The hotel maid had already come and gone. It was hours yet before someone would bring up dinner. "Go away," Hammett muttered, taking a pencil from behind his ear to mark a typographical error on the galley

13

page. Just now, nothing was more important than finishing his proof-reading and getting this manuscript back to the publisher. The studios were buzzing about the film rights. A big sale would set his finances straight; he'd blown a fortune the past few years living in a Beverly Hills mansion with a bowling alley in the basement and a swimming pool half the size of the Adriatic in the backyard . . . to say nothing of the limousines, fine wines, and the gentleman's gentleman. When the money finally ran low, he and Lily had come here to New York, where he threw himself into writing *The Thin Man*. Sometimes he worked sixteen or more hours straight. Now the novel was done, but for this final "going over."

More knocking at the door.

"Lillian, is that you?" he called. He wondered if she'd forgotten her key again.

A woman answered from beyond the door, but Hammett didn't recognize her voice and could not make out her words. He set the manuscript on the rug and pulled himself up from the couch.

"It's your past come to call," the woman continued.

He was in no mood for games. "Cut the crap," he said, opening the door.

"Hello, Sam," said Moira O'Shea, the redhead from his Black Falcon days.

He stepped back, speechless.

"Cat got your tongue? Come now, Sam. I haven't changed that much."

It was true, he thought, surprised that spending the past eleven years in a locked ward at the Patton State Hospital for the Criminally Insane had taken so little toll on her appearance. She was still a looker. Her cobalt blue eyes, which years before he had watched fill with tears (making him want to believe whatever lies she told him), glowed as brightly as before. And her body . . . In the book he'd described her as tall and high-breasted.[1] If anything, the years since he'd seen her had only filled her out more alluringly. "Hello, Moira."

"You look surprised, Sam."

Naturally, he'd followed her trial in San Francisco back in '22. She had played it just right—the failed suicide attempt immediately after her arrest, the tearful remorse on the witness stand four months later when she was deemed healthy enough to stand trial, the stories of childhood beatings . . .

"Well, aren't you going to invite me in?"

When he sent her over to the police—the night Gaspereaux was killed by his bodyguard and the whole Falcon business put to bed— he knew she could hang for her crimes, or at least get twenty years in the penitentiary. Such ruin didn't please him. But what choice did he have? Sure, she hadn't actually conspired to murder his partner, who was alive and well (Hammett had invented that part for *The Maltese Falcon*), but she *had* conspired in the killing of the ship captain. And worse, as far as Hammett was concerned, she had plotted separately with both Cletus Gaspereaux and Emil Madrid to use Hammett as a dupe in her attempt to acquire the jeweled statuette. How could he trust her after that, however good she'd made him feel during the weeks they'd been together? Christ, he'd temporarily left his new wife for her. She'd changed his life. And he'd meant the things he'd said to her. But after her skein of deceit unraveled, what option was left him but to hand her over?

"It's not polite to leave a lady standing in the hallway," she continued.

When the jury brought back a verdict of not guilty by reason of insanity, he was relieved, though he knew it meant one day she would show up like this on his doorstep. Over the years, he considered a hundred responses to a hundred possible scenarios, which ranged from the romantic to the nostalgic to the vengeful to the murderous. Yet now he felt unprepared. "Come in," he said, because he could think of nothing else to say.

"Thanks, Sam."

She slipped past him and through the doorway, leaving a scent of lilac that he remembered from their nights together. The scent induced a warmth in his body and a lightness in his head—the last thing he needed right now. "You're looking well, Moira."

"You too, Sam. Or should I call you 'Dashiell' now?"

"Whichever," he said. "My old friends still call me Sam."

"Do I qualify as an old friend?"

He nodded, though he wasn't quite sure what word actually described what Moira was to him.

"Thanks, Sam."

"How long have you been out?"

"Three weeks."

"And you're here already? You work fast."

"I always did. Or don't you remember?"

He remembered plenty. But that didn't mean he wanted to talk about it. "These days, I'm not the easiest man to find."

"Oh, it wasn't difficult." She dropped her handbag onto the coffee table. "You're famous. There's no hiding out for you. Not since . . . Let's see, what name did you give to that book, our little true history? Oh yes. *The Maltese Falcon*. No, Sam. There'll be no more hiding for you, ever again. Congratulations on your success."

He shrugged.

"I've followed your career with great interest." She crossed the room to a spot where the light from outside played flatteringly about her auburn hair. Hammett suspected that she instinctively knew as much about glamour lighting as all but the most experienced gaffers in Hollywood. "I read about you in the newspapers and magazines," she continued. "I especially enjoyed the gossip columns that described your evenings out with starlets or how much alcohol you and Scott Fitzgerald put away together on a good night. Unfortunately though, your books were never allowed inside the hospital. Too violent, they said. But on the train east I read all of them. I hardly slept. Wow, that

Red Harvest is a real shoot-em-up. Makes our little gunplay in San Francisco seem like a child's game."

"It was no child's play, Moira."

"Oh, sorry. I almost forgot." Her tone grew mocking: "Let's see, how did you put it? 'It's bad business to let a killer get away with it. Bad for every detective everywhere.' Wasn't that you speaking, Sam?"

He didn't answer.

"Or was that what your character, Sam Spade, said in your novel?" she asked. "Or did both of you say it? See, I'm not sure anymore if what I remember of San Francisco is what actually happened or if I've confused it with what happens in your oh-so-famous book, which kept me on the edge of my seat all the way from Kansas City to Chicago."

"I get confused sometimes myself, Moira."

"Well, you sure didn't 'play the sap' for me."

"Not yet at least."

She surveyed the suite. "Nice digs. This writing thing's put you in the chips."

"Unfortunately, I'm not one to hold on to money for very long."

"You don't hold to anything for long, Sam."

He thought of his writing, to which he considered himself devoted. He thought, too, of Lillian. "I've changed, Moira."

"Nobody changes."

"Not even you?"

"Well, I may be the exception, because I've had eleven years of professional psychiatric help."

"That's a long time." He closed the door and moved into the room.

She fixed him with an ironic smile. "Oh, time flies inside a hospital for the criminally insane. There are so many diverting activities. Yachting, alpine skiing. The hospital attendants are practically like cruise directors. Hasn't everyone who's ever done time in such a place told you the same thing?"

"You avoided hard time," Hammett said.

Her shoulders stiffened, her expression hardening. "You try living in a psychiatric ward for eleven hours, let alone eleven years. You might not want to argue about what is or isn't 'hard.'"

"Look, I didn't enjoy sending you over, Moira."

"I don't blame you for what you did."

"No?"

She stepped toward him. "But you could have visited once or twice."

"They told me you couldn't have any visitors who'd been involved in the crimes."

She looked into his eyes. "You mean you tried to visit?"

It was true that she'd meant something to him. "I was curious."

She went to him. "Oh Sam, I never forgot you. Not for a day. And you haven't forgotten me either?"

He grabbed her hard by the shoulders, pulling her close. "No, I haven't forgotten who you are." She turned her face up to kiss him, but he only pulled her tighter, running his hands over her body to feel for hidden weapons.

"You're hurting me," she said.

He pushed her away and moved to her handbag, which he picked up and dumped onto the coffee table. A small pistol clattered to rest along with a silver compact, two tubes of lipstick, a key, a book of matches, two cigarettes, a handkerchief, a comb, a letter, two five-dollar bills and seventy-four cents in coin. He picked up the gun.

"What do you expect?" she asked. "It's a dangerous world. I have to protect myself."

He said nothing.

"You don't think I brought the gun to use on you, do you?"

"Did you?"

"If I'd come here to kill you, Sam, I'd have brought a larger caliber gun."

He leveled the gun at her. "A small caliber can do plenty of damage if it's aimed properly."

"What's gotten into you, Sam?"

He wondered the same. "Why are you here, Moira?"

"You have no ideas?"

"Plenty," he said. "But it'd be a lot faster if you spelled it out."

She smiled. "Faster isn't always better. Not when it comes to romance."

"Romance? That word means different things to different people."

"You know what it means to me, Sam."

He nodded. "That's what worries me."

She turned and crossed back to the window, this time looking out. Hammett had spent a lot of time these past weeks in the same spot, gazing down Fifth Avenue or across to the park. He looked her up and down, wanting to go to her and touch her—despite everything. He suspected she'd offer no resistance if he put his arms around her, pressing his lips to the back of her neck, and then led her into the other room and onto the bed where he might lose himself in the past as well as the present. The fantasy suggested he could disengage himself from her before her darker motives made it too late—but he knew reality didn't work that way. There was no such thing as a free lunch. Still, she was the sexiest woman he'd ever known, and he'd known more than a few.

"Sam, I've come here," she said without turning around, "because you once said to me that all we've got is the fact that maybe you love me and maybe I love you."

She was playing for high stakes, he thought. "I didn't say that, Moira. That's a line of dialogue from out of the book. Spade says it."

She turned to him, her eyes alight. "But it was what you were thinking."

"Who can remember that long ago?"

"I can, for one."

He steeled himself. He knew the wisest thing to do was to get out of here. "Look, let's go down the street and get a drink," he suggested. The last thing he needed was for Lily to return from the library or wherever she'd gone this afternoon and find him here alone with a voluptuous redhead who happened to be hell-bent on proclaiming their love for one another (assuming Moira wasn't harboring even more destructive intentions).

"Who is this Lillian woman I've read about in the gossip columns?" she asked, as if she knew what he was thinking. "I understand the two of you are as good as married."

"Marriage doesn't suit me. But yes, Lily and I are together."

Her eyes dropped. When she looked up they glistened. He was reminded how good she was, a real pro from the old school. "I've been gone a long time," she said, opening her hands to him as if conferring a pardon. "I'm glad this Lily woman has been here for you, Sam."

Has been here rather than *is* here? He didn't like what her choice of verb tense suggested. He couldn't let this spin out of control. "Let's get out of here," he said.

"Why?"

He needed the reassurance of a public place. "There's a nice bar in the lobby. We can get something to drink."

"Have them bring drinks up, if you're so thirsty," she said.

"We're getting out of here, Moira."

She didn't move. "A little common decency from you would be nice," she snapped. "Considering all that's transpired between us."

"I intended to pay for the drinks."

"Damn you, Sam! Have you no feelings?"

"What do you want?"

"I want to go back in time and do it all over again."

"The same?"

"Why would anyone go back in time just to do it again the same?" she asked. "You'd have to be crazy."

Exactly, thought Hammett.

"Forget the eleven years I spent in stir," she continued. "That hardly matters now. It hardly mattered then, as I'd already lost everything I cared about. Of course, you wouldn't understand, Sam. You lost nothing. But I lost the Falcon and I lost you."

"The Falcon was a fake, Moira."

"And you, Sam? Are you a fake?"

"I ask myself that question every day."

She grinned, chillingly. "I know you do, darling."

He didn't like the hint of smug menace.

She put her palms together at her lips, as if in prayer. "I don't blame you for sending me over to the cops."

"You already said that."

"But whether I blame you or not doesn't count for much." She brushed at her hair with one hand.

He didn't follow.

"Look," she said, stepping toward him. "I'm a duplicitous bitch. Isn't that right, Sam?" She didn't wait for an answer. "I'm a state-sanctioned sociopath. So it can be no surprise that I *naturally* regard your betrayal as being just a logical consequence in the big lie that is life. See, in that light, how can I blame you for what you did? You're a man. It would be like blaming a bishop for moving diagonally on a chessboard—it's just what bishops do. At least, that's how it's bound to appear to a state-sanctioned sociopath like me."

"We aren't chess pieces, Moira."

"Hah!" she laughed. "You think not?"

"I was sorry about the way things turned out . . ."

She cut him off with a wave of her hand. "Don't waste your breath, Sam. Apologizing to me counts for nothing. Can't you see that?"

He stepped toward her. "I wasn't playing you, Moira. Remember? You were the one on the grift."

"Yes! That's what I'm saying. I was the duplicitous bitch. That's not up for debate."

"So what the hell do you want from me?"

She took a deep, calming breath and then ran her hands down the front of her dress, as if straightening wrinkles in the fabric that were not there. "Since my status as sociopath effectively eliminates any chance of my either truly forgiving or condemning you, then perhaps you should consider a different standard in the question of your behavior."

He shook his head no. "I have no further questions about that."

"Well, I have a question for you. It's about your oh-so-famous novel, Mr. Hammett."

"This isn't a ladies' book circle."

She ignored him. "Tell me, Mr. Author, why your character Sam Spade gives over the woman he loves at the end of the book."

Hammett sighed. "You know damn well."

"Tell me," she demanded.

"Because she's a duplicitous bitch."

"No!" she shouted. "That's not why!"

He said nothing.

"He gives her over because she murdered his partner," she said. "It's right there on the page in black and white."

He couldn't deny that.

"But I did no such thing," she continued.

He stepped back, laughing. "It's a novel, Moira. It's called dramatic license."

"Your novel's hero is no real hero without that detail."

"What do you know about writing a goddamn book?"

"You put in the bit about the dead partner because you *wish* you'd been as justified in doing what you did to me as your character was in what he did to . . . what'd you call her?"

"Brigid O'Shaughnessy."

"Yeah, her."

He sighed. "Is this what the psychiatrists have filled your head with, Moira?"

"No."

Where was his damn hat? He needed to get her out of here. Now.

"It's your book, Sam. I didn't write it. But I can read it."

"You don't know me, Moira. You never did."

She looked away. "Why are you being cruel to me? How does that serve you?"

"I'm just being truthful," he said.

"As you were always truthful?"

He picked up his hat. "I don't usually see much angle to lying."

"So you meant all the things you said to me, years ago?" she asked, a disarming vulnerability suddenly in her voice.

Yes, he had meant those things. "Look, I can't give you back the past, Moira. Nobody can."

"But if you could?"

He considered. "Sure, why not?"

"Then you don't hate me?"

"I don't hate you."

"But you don't want me in your life?"

"My life is full-up."

"You mean full of that Lillian woman?"

"And my work."

She moved to the couch and sat down. "Ah, yes, you're quite the success these days."

He set his hat back down on the table. He wasn't going to get her out of here just yet. "Your encouragement meant a lot to me, Moira."

She laughed, bemused.

"No joke," he said.

"Wrong, Sam. A joke is exactly what it is. Your problem is that you don't know the punch line yet."

Hammett knew this: in his bed one night in '22—before the fullness of Moira's dark, conspiratorial nature became clear to him—she'd rested her head in the crook of his arm and confessed that she'd pilfered his case notes on the Black Falcon affair (then still embroiled in mystery) from his desk at the Pinkerton office. As her confession occurred only a few minutes after sex, Hammett's reaction was relaxed. She proceeded to tell him that the most important thing she gleaned from his notes was not any single piece of information, but the realization that he possessed a strong, straightforward prose style that not only served as something of an aphrodisiac for her but also suggested he might one day be wise to trade his Pinkerton-issued .38 for a typewriter. Hammett had always harbored this fantasy and admitted as much to her a few nights before, during a similarly intimate moment. But having dropped out of school at fourteen, he generally allowed himself only fleeting moments to indulge unlikely career changes. That night, however, Moira dug the dormant seed out of his brain and replanted it more deeply than ever, her erudition and worldliness serving to nurture the thing until it began to grow, then and there. Would the Falcon case have been Hammett's last were it not for her encouragement that night? How could he hate her, however dark their affair soon turned? "So what's the joke, Moira?"

"You are, Sam."

"I don't understand."

She stood up from the couch and took a long breath. "I don't mean to be evil."

"Who said anything about 'evil'?"

"But I can't help it," she continued. "It's just in me." She looked at her hands, helplessly. "I'm cursed."

"Cursed?"

"You can't deny that my life has been cursed. Or that I've cursed the lives of all those I ever touched. Do you believe that a curse can be handed down from mother to daughter?"

At last, he recognized the words. It was dialogue he'd written. "You can stop now, Moira."

"What do you mean?"

"You're quoting from *The Dain Curse*."

"Am I?" she said. "It's just so natural. No wonder the critics like you. Where *do* you get your material, Mr. Hammett?"

"*The Dain Curse* is strictly a work of fiction."

"Like *The Maltese Falcon*, right?"

"That's different."

"Oh, I forgot," she said. "You're a novelist. Your business is with 'souls and what goes on in them.'"

She was quoting him again—this time it was a different character from *The Dain Curse*, a writer of esoteric tales and the novel's villain—not a character Hammett wanted to encourage Moira to think of just now as his doppelganger. "I'm impressed you're such a close reader of my books, Moira. But let's not get carried away."

"You'd like me to just disappear again from your life?" she asked.

She was all over the place. "Look, why don't you just tell me what you want?"

She turned in a slow circle, taking in the room. "Maybe a little something to acknowledge our time together."

"Can you be more specific?"

"What if I asked you to love me?"

"I already did that, Moira. It didn't go well. Got any other suggestions?"

"Try it again?"

He shook his head no.

"Well," she said, gathering her arms about herself. "I expected as much. Still, you might at least offer me a souvenir."

"A souvenir of what?"

"Of what brought us together in the first place."

"Crime brought us together, Moira."

"You bastard."

"You mean the Falcon?" he asked.

"That's an idea."

"You know damn well the thing never turned up. Hell, you know more about it than I ever did."

"What became of the counterfeit Falcon, the one without the jewels?"

He turned to his desk, where the black, stone statuette sat beside his typewriter. "It's right there."

"Yes. Lovely."

"It was entered in evidence in Emil Madrid's trial," he said. "I bought it afterwards at a police auction for ten bucks."

"That's a lot of money for a rock."

"Call me sentimental."

With her fingertips, she traced cryptic patterns in a lace doily set atop the back of a wing chair. "On the other hand, imagine all the plotting and betrayal and killing associated with that little bird. And in the end it sells for a measly ten bucks."

"Life is full of irony."

"Cruelty, I'd call it," she said.

"It's just a rock."

"Will you give it to me?"

"Why?"

"Old times' sake."

He laughed. "And that'll make us square, Moira?"

"We'll never be square. But I want the statuette."

"It hardly even looks like a bird."

"If I wanted a bird I'd go to a taxidermist."

He started toward the statuette to give it to her but something stopped him. "I like the damn thing, Moira." He turned back to her. "And I don't like feeling strong-armed, even if it's only for a rock."

She went to the coffee table, scooping her scattered items into the handbag. "May I please have my gun back?"

He emptied the bullets into his palm, then handed her the gun.

"I didn't really come here to win you back, lover," she said.

"Good."

"Oh, maybe I'd have gone with you if you'd asked nicely, but I didn't really expect that. No, Sam, I came here for the bird."

He looked again at the statuette. "That thing? Why?"

"It's not what it appears to be, Sam. It's no ordinary rock. It's kind of . . . what's a good word? Enchanted?"

He laughed.

"I'm not joking, Sam."

Hammett wondered if Moira's commitment to the psychiatric hospital had been more than a legal ruse; maybe a wheel or pulley actually had slipped in her mind after she attempted to hang herself at the city jail in San Francisco. Maybe the jury had been right to find her insane (though at the time of the Black Falcon affair she'd seemed plenty lucid). He couldn't figure her angle. But that didn't mean there wasn't one.

She asked: "Do you know the thirteenth-century poem *Perceval* by Chrétien de Troyes?"

His face expressed his thought: "What the hell?"

She repeated herself.

"I've heard of it," he said.

"And Wolfram von Eschenbach's *Parzival*, another epic poem?"

"Sure, but I haven't read either. Why?"

Might the psychiatric facility in California have been overly optimistic in its assessment of Moira's sanity? Suddenly, he wanted more than ever to be out on the street with the scent of diesel and gasoline exhaust, the sound of automobile horns and shouted voices—anything to take him from the quiet of this suite, where he'd been holed up too many days and nights these past months and where such apparitions as Moira seemed bound to appear from time to time. He realized that over the years he'd come to believe she was as fictional as the O'Shaughnessy character he based upon her.

"The two poems are the original tales of Percival," she said. "Percival was a Knight of the Round Table."

"You studied continental literature in the psychiatric ward?"

"Don't patronize me, please." She held up her hands to stop him from saying more. "Look, I knew about all this before the hospital.

Before I ever got to San Francisco with the bird! I knew about it in Hong Kong and even before that. Understand? Emil knew, too. That's why we got involved, years before you entered the picture."

"Involved in what?"

"The Black Falcon affair."

"You've lost me, Moira."

"Oh, you've been 'lost' for some time, Sam. Much longer than you know. From the beginning, actually. But don't feel too bad. The Big Man was as ill-informed as you. And he'd gotten into the mix years before I did. Emil and I never told him what we learned, never told him the whole story."

"What story?"

"The Big Man believed to his dying day we were merely pursuing a jeweled bird."

"Weren't you?"

She shook her head no. "We never told him the truth, because we knew he'd never believe us."

"Believe what?"

"I have something to show you." She opened her handbag and withdrew an envelope. "This correspondence explains the thing better than I can." She removed three typed pages, handing Hammett the middle sheet. "You don't need to see the name of the man who wrote this or any of the personal stuff at the beginning."

Despite his better judgment, he took the paper.

"Well, read it," she said.

He was already deeper into this than he wanted to be; nonetheless, he read the page:

as I know you're already aware, Moira. But I have confirmed it through the sources you recommended when we were together in the unmentionable place (from which you'll soon be released, at which time we

can at last be together in an unobserved embrace!).
Here goes: It is true that both Chrétien de Troyes and
Wolfram von Eschenbach based their poems on earlier
Welsh legends now collected under the title The Mabinogion, which dates from the time the first Crusaders
returned to the British Isles from the Holy Land. It is
likewise true that in these earliest sources, the Grail is
identified not as a chalice or cup but as a stone, called
"lapsit exillas," which translates either as "stone from
heaven" or "stone from exile." Wolfram, who had been
a Crusader, writes that the stone possessed magical,
wish-fulfilling properties.

Hammett stopped.

She nodded, portentously. "You can look it up. A black stone.
Beginning to see?"

"No."

She motioned to the pages in his hand. "Read on."

Arguing with her seemed pointless.

The Crusaders had acquired the stone in the Middle
East. There, it had long been believed to contain supernatural powers, which were ascribed to other, older
religious sources. Ghral means "holy stone" in Persian-
Arabic. Some historians suggest that the stone may be
related to the famed philosopher's stone of alchemy.

Hammett considered what new skills of misdirection Moira might
have acquired living among the criminally insane. One might derive a
whole new school of confidence games from such sources, he thought.

"Moira, what's this supposed to mean?"

"The story you put in your book about the Knights of Rhodes is
not entirely accurate."

"I wasn't writing a history textbook."

"You suggested they created the jeweled Falcon in tribute to King Charles V."

"That's right."

"No, Sam, that's wrong."

"What are you getting at?"

"Did it ever occur to you that the Knights created a jeweled Falcon merely to serve as a diversion from their real treasure, which was actually an obsidian stone recovered from the Holy Land by members of their order a century before?"

"No, it never occurred to me."

"Too bad for you."

He shook his head and returned to the page:

The Crusaders interpreted the source of the stone's mystical attributes after their own fashion, elaborating on its origins until its essential characteristic, its redeeming power, became mixed up with the crucifixion and another object altogether, the chalice from which Christ drank at the Last Supper. In this manner, the black stone eventually ceased to be a part of the Grail story, though it was the source. However, the actual stone didn't disappear from the planet. Now, mere proximity

The page ended. Hammett handed it back to Moira. "This guy ought to get a job writing for the Hearst papers."

"He's a full, tenured professor." She glanced over the third typed page until she found what she was looking for. "And the invention of the Christian Grail mythology," she read, "arose not only because of the prevailing theology, which disavowed any object of supernatural power that wasn't related to Christianity, but also as a kind of 'cover story' for the existence of the stone, which eventually disappeared from history."

"And you believe this?" he asked.

She looked at him. "Possessing the stone changes a person's life."

"It grants wishes?"

"In a manner of speaking, yes."

He looked away. "The man who wrote this letter refers to an 'unmentionable place.'"

"You know damn well what he means."

"You met him in the psychiatric hospital?"

"Damn you, Sam! He merely confirmed the story because he's a scientist of impeccable distinction and knew all the right sources. But I was familiar with the truth long before I met him. I already told you that, you bastard. This is not some psych-ward fantasy."

"Jesus, it's the twentieth century, Moira. A magical talisman?"

"Please, Sam, don't speak to me so roughly." She put her hand to her heart. "I'm not the same as when you knew me. I can't take your abusive ways. The years have been hard."

He'd had his fill of it.

"You used to comfort me, remember?" she asked.

"I hate to see you making a fool of yourself, Moira."

"You're the fool!" she snapped, her fragility replaced by rage.

"Look, if this thing is so valuable why would I just give it to you?" he asked. "You know as well as anyone how a con works, Moira. You don't spell out the score for the *mark*."

"This isn't a con."

"You haven't answered my question."

"You'll give me the statuette because you claim not to believe the story."

He smiled. "I *don't* believe it."

"You *can't* believe it, because you're incapable of even considering that the success you've had these past eleven years is due to your coincidental possession of that stone sitting there on your desk. You want to believe it's all been about you and your talent."

He shook his head and gestured with his hands that he was at a loss as to how a sane man might answer her ravings.

She continued: "But the only way you can ever prove to me, or to yourself, that you truly don't believe what I've told you about that stone is to give it to me here and now."

He'd been trained to speak to criminals. Lunatics were another thing altogether.

"You're a coward, Sam. And as a writer, you're a fraud."

He crossed the room to his desk and picked up the black statuette. "This is really what you've come for?"

"You don't have the balls to give it to me, Sam. Do you know why?"

He waited.

"Because deep inside you *do* believe the story I told you about it. Come on, I know who you are, Sam. I haven't forgotten the stories of your childhood, the ones you told me on nights we spent together in bed. Whatever your pretensions now, you'll never really be anything more than an uneducated gumshoe from the wrong side of the tracks. Novelist, hah! Fourteen-year-old dropout is more like it. Ignorant hustler turned strikebreaking son-of-a-bitch who's come now to think of himself as a politically enlightened, literary gentleman. Of all things! Come on, Sam, where do you think the jazz to write those books of yours came from?"

"I worked at it, Moira," he said.

She offered mock applause. "Let's hear it for Horatio Alger."

"Sorry, but my case notes were always good. You weren't the only one who said so. And they preceded the goddamn statuette."

She laughed. "Your case notes only proved that you weren't a complete illiterate, which served to place you in the exclusive company of about twenty million other office stiffs all staining their shirt cuffs with leaked ink at their pathetic little desks."

"Why am I even discussing this bullshit with you?"

"You know damn well why you're justifying yourself, Sam."

"It's time for you to leave."

She shook her head as if suddenly sympathetic. "Ah, Sam . . . I'm actually sorry that everything I've said is true. Surely you've wondered about it yourself. And now you know the answer. The punch line to the joke. Now, you know that your having the bird these past years explains *everything*, right down to your being ensconced here at the Pierre in a suite fit for a movie star."

He shook his head and laughed.

"Go ahead, pretend," she said, stepping toward him.

Instinctively, he stepped back.

"I understand that your ego requires you to deny the truth, darling," she continued. "But deep inside you know that everything I've told you is true. Why else would you fuss over giving away an ugly black rock? Especially since that's all it'll take to rid you of your 'Moira problem' forever."

"I'm supposed to take this seriously?"

She crossed her arms. "I just want the bird. It'll change everything for me, as it did for you."

"Then take it."

She took another step toward him and gently removed the statuette from his hands. "You're right, Sam. It hardly looks like a falcon."

"If you'd wanted a bird, you'd have gone to a taxidermist."

She put the statuette into her handbag. "You won't miss it much. Wait, that's not true. You're going to miss it a lot. Even more than you missed me." She turned to go.

He took her hand to stop her, but when she turned to him he didn't know what to say.

"Are you going to ask me to stay?" she prodded, doubtless already knowing the answer.

Of course he wasn't.

"I didn't think so," she said, lucid and composed. "Still, Sam, I want you to know I didn't come here merely to be cruel to you. Just honest, for once. I hope you make the best of . . ." She didn't finish the sentence.

Then she was gone.

He paced the room for a while. He threw back two drinks and concluded that his agitation was natural—seeing Moira again after all these years. . . . He'd loved her once, so it was no laughing matter to see how low her delusions had sunk her. He would hardly be human if he was not shaken by the pathos of her seeming to actually believe a supernatural yarn unworthy even of a crackpot hack like Sax Rohmer—a premise so fantastic that it wouldn't make it past the most callow editor at *Black Mask* magazine. Still, he knew that if this was the worst of her return he should count himself lucky. She might have come back with muscle or real heat. He drank a third and fourth whiskey before settling onto the sofa to pick up where he'd left off with his proofreading of *The Thin Man*. He shuffled the pages into order and forced his eyes onto the page, resolved not let Moira throw him off stride. But now his characters Nick and Nora Charles seemed less witty than they'd seemed before her arrival. After a while, he stopped reading and looked up— the room still smelled of lilac.

When Lily arrived a half hour later she asked, "How's your work going?"

He didn't know how to answer.

"What's that smell?" she asked, putting down her shopping bags and looking around the room. "I don't see any flowers. Is it somebody's perfume?"

"A woman from my past . . ."

"Stop," she interrupted, holding her palm out like a traffic cop. "I don't want to hear about it."

"It was the O'Shea woman from the Black Falcon case," he said.

Lily's lips pursed.

"Nothing happened," he offered, reassuringly. "She just came and went."

Lily still looked confused.

"The redhead," he added for clarification.

"Brigid O'Shaughnessy?"

"The real one, dear."

She narrowed her eyes. "She's out of prison?"

"Mental hospital. But I think they may have let her out too soon."

Lily crossed the room and poured a whiskey from the crystal decanter, a gift from Sam Goldwyn. "Is she still dangerous?"

"I don't think so." He finished his drink and then moved toward Lily, holding his glass out to her to refill.

She poured. "If you get us killed by some deranged broad from your disreputable past I'll never forgive you, Hammett."

"Drink up, Lillian. She's not going to get us killed."

"I swear, I'll torment you beyond the grave," she continued. "Things are going too well for both of us now."

She was right.

Yes, things were good, and he too had great hopes for the future.

TIME MAGAZINE

FEBRUARY 17, 1936
LENI REIFENSTAHL

It has been three weeks since Hammett and Hellman moved into the suite at the Beverly Wilshire Hotel, but still he has failed to get his room organized just as he likes it. And so how is he supposed to get any work done? Naturally, there is the question of space. The couple's books rise in piles on the floor like stalagmites in a cave. And at this time of year, with east-facing windows, the room might as well be subterranean for all the natural light it provides in the afternoons. He has tried drawing the blinds after lunch to pretend it's night. But here in Hollywood the nights (even the imagined ones) are never good for work—they offer too many enticing distractions. Meantime, Lily has had good luck just by sitting up in the couple's bed in the other room, scratching away on a legal pad. Her first play was a hit and her second is now coming to her almost as fast as she can move her pencil. He doesn't hold it against her. But as he contemplates rearranging the furniture in his study yet again, he thinks that the least she could do is offer to help him with the heavy lifting. He sure as hell doesn't want to call the bell staff to move the furniture—it would be the fourth time in five days. They'll think he's gone mad up here. He settles himself on a loveseat and takes a deep breath, worn out from a day of doing nothing. A pile of blank paper sits on the desk beside his typewriter, which he has fitted with a new typing ribbon and for which he has purchased a half dozen other ribbons, all sitting now in their small boxes in a shopping bag on a table near the gray window. A magazine sits on the floor—this week's *Time*, how did he miss it? Determined to stay in this goddamn room until at least four o'clock (a bargain he has made with himself), he picks up the magazine. The Nazi bitch Leni Reifenstahl is on the cover, absurdly posed half-naked on snow skis. He doesn't feel like reading this. He tosses the magazine across the cluttered room and goes to the phone, calling down to the bell staff to come upstairs and help him move the furniture again.

While we may dismiss the postulation of the "fantastical"
from any one character as being mere psychotic ramblings,
if a second character suggests support for the "insupportable"
the reader will begin to reconsider what he or she thought
possible in the world of your story.

—Dashiell Hammett, from an article published in
The Young Writer's Monthly Journal, August 1927

SAN FRANCISCO, 1936

The first light of morning slipped through a crack in the blinds, illuminating for the just-awakening Hammett a small, beaded chandelier directly above the bed. The cut glass reflected droplets of light on the ceiling; otherwise, the room was dark. He didn't recall where he was but the bed was warm and he was sleepy and so he closed his eyes again. When he opened them the room had grown lighter. He discerned the shapely thigh of a naked companion, which had emerged at some unknown hour from beneath the tangle of bedcovers to rest now across his knees. Her arm was draped over his chest and her head rested against his rib cage. Had they been wrestlers, she could rightfully claim a pin. At first, he didn't recall who was draped across him. When he remembered, he sighed and knew he would not be getting back to sleep.

Evie LeFabre.

She had come to work as Hammett's secretary at the Pinkerton Detective Agency in 1920. She was eighteen years old then, which made her thirty-four now, he figured. By that age any woman was responsible for her misadventures. Except that Evie wasn't just "any woman." Hammett had always thought of her as something of a kid sister—this despite her lithe, athletic body, the proximity to which had only occasionally tested his self-discipline in the Pinkerton office, where she typed his letters, answered his phone calls, rubbed the tension out of his shoulders, and rolled his cigarettes with her nimble fingers. Now, he couldn't help but feel a twinge of guilt, making him wish he could jump out of bed and go downstairs to distract himself with a cup of coffee spiked with a little whiskey.

Evie stirred beside him.

He froze beneath her.

She settled once more into sleep, her right hand moving across his chest to rest on his left shoulder.

The night before in the taxi cab, returning from dinner and drinking, she'd told him she loved him. She said she always had. At the time, he told himself it was only the gin talking. In response, he touched her face with his fingertips—a handy gesture that was simultaneously tender and noncommittal. The subject of love didn't arise again in the car or in Evie's apartment, though Hammett knew that having once been broached it provided an implicit context to all that followed, whether he acknowledged it or not. Most times, he wouldn't care. He'd tell himself it was part of the foreplay, to be forgotten by the morning's light. But with Evie . . . Once or twice in bed the previous night he felt angry that she'd introduced such terms to the relationship—all the women he slept with these days (excluding Lily, of course) knew better than to confuse issues. He inched away from Evie, careful to move in time with her gentle exhalations, in hopes that he might slide out from under her and off the bed without jostling the mattress, which he recalled had squeaky springs.

"Sam?" she whispered, still half-asleep.

"Shhh," he said, holding his breath.

"There're coins in my pocket," she muttered meaninglessly in her sleep. She didn't open her eyes, but eased against him. After a moment, her breathing regained the regularity of a deeper sleep. He lifted his head from the pillow, but he could not see her face—only the top of her head, where the part in her soft, tussled brown hair ran a crazy zigzag.

Poor kid.

Before last night, he'd not seen or heard from her since '22, just after the Black Falcon affair came to its bloody conclusion and he left the detective business to pursue writing fiction. Evie too had resigned from the Pinkerton Agency at that time, cleaning out her desk before the ink was dry on Hammett's resignation letter; however, unlike Hammett, who had remained in San Francisco for a few years, Evie disappeared. Hammett was surprised the previous day at the mortuary to spot her among the mourners for SFPD detective Tom Paulson, an old acquaintance who had dropped dead at his desk in the homicide room while eating a meatball sandwich. Evie was seated on the opposite side of the mortuary chapel. When Hammett caught her eye, she blushed and turned away. In the reception hall outside the viewing chapel, which was crowded with mourners, Hammett approached her.

She looked different. Not bad, but different.

At first, he thought the change was a mere matter of maturity. At twenty, she'd possessed the lingering scent of grassy fields played in as a child and the manner of one who hides skinned knees beneath the folds of her well-pressed dress. But now she was a woman. It pleased him. However, when he looked at her eyes, he discerned an expression he hadn't seen in the two years they worked together. Distress. Time alone didn't leave such marks. He had assumed she'd left the detective agency to seek in its place a neat house with a white picket fence. But something had gone wrong. A bad marriage? Too much drink? He opened his arms, into which she fit quite nicely.

"Nice to see you again," he said.

She nodded. "Of course, it's a shame it's under such sad circumstances."

Hammett agreed, but he wasn't all that sad. The last time he'd seen Paulson was seven years before, when the cop arrived unexpectedly at Hammett's apartment on Post Street to congratulate him on the publication of *The Maltese Falcon*. Paulson had kidded Hammett for a lack of originality in naming one of the detectives in the book "Tom Poulhaus," who Paulson mistakenly believed was based on him. Hammett didn't tell Paulson that despite the similarity of the names, the Poulhaus character was actually modeled on a detective Hammett had known in Baltimore when he first started working for the Pinkertons. He didn't disillusion the detective, having learned not to antagonize hard-ass cops, who were never as simple to manage in real life as his character Sam Spade's irreverence suggested in fiction. Now, Paulson was dead. He was buried with the honors due an officer killed in the line of duty; of course, a meatball sandwich wasn't ordinarily considered a deadly weapon, but Paulson had become one of the department's best known figures and organizing a rousing send-off was good for police morale. The police commissioner himself invited Hammett to Paulson's memorial service.

Evie LeFabre wasn't supposed to figure in any of it.

"I didn't know you were acquainted with Paulson, Evie," Hammett observed in the mortuary.

"I wasn't."

"Then why are you here?"

"Because I thought you might be here, Sam."

From the first day Evie came to work at the agency, she had nursed a crush on Hammett. He knew she was aroused by observing—as his messenger or confidante—the love affairs he enjoyed with single office girls who worked near the agency in downtown banks or with women who came into the agency seeking proof that their husbands were philanderers or even with the wives of other agency operatives, who Evie sometimes had to avoid in the break room for fear she might accidentally reveal their cuckoldry with a misplaced word or gesture. She made a good pal for Hammett, offering advice on which of his lovers best suited his needs at any given time and sometimes suggesting maneuvers by which he might seduce one or another new girl. But he never made a play for Evie, which is how they remained friends—at least until the conclusion of the Black Falcon affair when Hammett handed over to the police Moira O'Shea, whose criminality Evie naively believed should be ignored in favor of romance. Disillusioned, Evie didn't speak to him for the last three days of her employment. Then she disappeared.

"I was at the dedication of the new wing at the library a while back," she said. "I remembered how much time you used to spend there and thought maybe you'd be invited to speak or something, considering all your literary success."

He shook his head no. "If you wanted to see me, why didn't you just write to me?"

"I didn't want to seek you out, Sam. That was something I couldn't do. I needed to just run into you, sort of accidentally."

"But if you came here looking for me . . ."

"Don't ask me to make sense, please."

"OK."

"Do you ever hear from Mike?" she asked.

Mike Arnette, his old partner. "No, last I heard he was still with the Pinkertons, in Denver. But I'm not sure. He doesn't return my letters. Not since *The Maltese Falcon*. I don't think he appreciated the Miles Archer character being murdered at the beginning of the book. But hell, it's a work of fiction. You'd think he'd be on to that sort of thing. Doesn't take a PhD in Literature."

"Are you writing a new book?"

Nothing he'd managed to put on the page had worked out these past three years. One shit start after another. No matter—something would develop. Once, writing had come easily. He trusted it would be easy again. The problem was just that there'd been too damn many distractions lately—the *Thin Man* movies and the radio adaptations of old work, about which the studio and the networks were always bothering him with questions and consultations (well paid, of course), and then there was Lily's play, for which he'd commented on draft after draft, and then all the hullabaloo in New York that followed its Broadway success. "No, I'm not writing anything new just now."

"Will you buy me a drink?" Evie asked.

"How about dinner?"

"Sure."

He helped her with her coat, looking around the walnut paneled main room of the mortuary. "This is the joint where we said our good-byes to Cletus Gaspereaux, isn't it?"[2]

"Yes, it is," she said brusquely, turning away.

He wondered if she was still sore about the old Falcon case. Evie was never cut out for the mortal rough-and-tumble of working with the Pinks—even if her actual job consisted primarily of typing up case notes. "Listen, Evie, I know my handing Moira O'Shea over to the cops bothered you. I know you think I used her, betrayed her."

Evie shook her head no, but her expression remained pained. "What you did was right, Sam. I understand that now. Moira was dangerous and needed to be put away, whatever you might once have felt for her, whatever you might once have told her, whatever you made her believe."

"That woman only ever believed what served her purposes."

"I understand, Sam." She looked up at him, her eyes brightening. "I've grown up in the years since you last saw me. I understand it all now."

He didn't understand it *all* himself. But he was glad to hear Evie had come around. "Yeah?"

She smiled. "Didn't you say something about getting something to eat? Are you still a patron of John's Grill?"

"Always. Why wouldn't I be?"

"You're a famous author now. You can eat anywhere."

He shrugged off the suggestion.

"Afterwards, maybe we can do the town together?" she asked.

He had nothing else planned. "Sure."

Now, as the bedroom grew lighter and Evie's sleeping body grew heavier against his own, Hammett wondered how he could have thought their evening would end any place but in bed. However, by the dim light of the bar in John's Grill—as Henry the bartender poured a scotch for his old customer Sam and a gin for Evie—Hammett hadn't yet trained his eye on her. It wasn't until they settled into a booth and ordered their porterhouse steaks that he took note of the way her breasts pressed against the fabric of her neatly ironed dress.

They didn't discuss the Black Falcon case over dinner.

Nor did Evie account for her disappearance in 1922 or where she'd been since then.

He didn't press her.

Rather, she pressed him, wanting to hear about his exciting turn of fortune since they last met—the short stories that had established his reputation in the pulp magazines as a master of detective fiction, followed by the publication of his best selling novels and his time in Hollywood. "And you've met movie stars there?" she asked.

He'd met many movie stars, whose private lives he described to her in detail well into the dessert course, which for Evie was apple pie à la mode and for Hammett was a brandy.

"And you live in a mansion?" she asked.

Actually, he and Lily were living now in a suite in the Beverly Wilshire Hotel. "I live comfortably."

"And you're here now with *me*?"

"You're worth the whole damn bunch of those Hollywood girls." By now, he was a little liquored-up, but he was still sober enough to know it was more than just the liquor speaking.

"You're my Sam."

He looked at her. She was no starlet; a screen test would reveal the ordinary bone structure of her face, the thinness of her lips, the hairdo that was five years out of date, the figure that was feminine and firm but less than perfect. Still, she possessed *something*. Was it sincerity? No, she'd been dodging his questions all night. Nor was it innocence as the hardness of her gaze, when it came to rest on one or another of the men and women who entered John's Grill, suggested she had endured much ill experience. "It's your turn now, Evie."

"For what?"

"To tell me what's happened to you since we last met."

"Didn't you say you were going to show me the town, Sam?"

"I plan to."

"Then let's get to it."

Hammett called the waiter to their table.

"Sir?" the waiter asked.

"Check, please."

"The boss says your money's no good here tonight, Mr. Hammett."

Hammett stood to shake the waiter's hand. "Funny, a guy can finally afford to buy a nice dinner and then he's not allowed to pay."

After dinner, Hammett and Evie visited some of his old haunts. First, the Dog Star Club, which was located in the basement of a textbook warehouse in the Tenderloin District. In '22, he'd brought Moira O'Shea here and over drinks had listened to her whole life story, which he later learned had been mostly lies; next, Hammett took Evie to The Thespian Club, which occupied the space beneath the stage at the abandoned California Street Theatre. He'd shadowed Emil Madrid here, just hours before the shooting began outside Gaspereaux's hotel. Of course, some of Hammett's favorite places were gone. The Regatta Club, "46" Club, The Circle Room. San Francisco was always a wide open city. Not long before, the owner of The Egyptian Room had been discovered stuffed in the mummy case that stood near the entrance to his nightclub, his throat slit.

"It was a bloody mess," Hammett said to Evie in a cab on their way to The Nighthawk Club, which they had decided would be their last stop of the night. "The 'King Tut' murder . . . Hell, it's like something out of a goddamn Philo Vance novel."

"Oh, S. S. Van Dine is no writer," Evie said.

"You got that right."

"He's not like you, Sam. You're a good writer, the real thing."

He wondered if she'd read his books. In particular, he wondered what she thought of *The Maltese Falcon*, which featured a character named "Effie Perrine," who had been modeled on her. He'd treated Effie's character sympathetically, depicting her as the only marginally "good-hearted" character in the book. However, by the story's end Effie is as disillusioned in her affections for Sam Spade as Evie had seemed to be for Samuel Hammett in the last of their Pinkerton days. He meant to ask Evie what she thought of the book. But in each of the nightclubs Hammett had been welcomed by old acquaintances with enthusiastic offers of free drinks and exuberant recollections of the "good old days."

"This is Polk and Eddy," the cab driver announced, pulling to the curb.

They climbed out of the cab and watched it pull away. Hammett took Evie's hand and led her up Polk Street.

She stopped.

"What is it?" he asked.

"I'm not who I used to be, Sam."

"None of us are."

She turned away.

He assumed the alcohol had begun to play with her emotions. She'd had a lot to drink. "Look, what do you say we don't go into the Nighthawk?" He didn't need any drunken scenes.

"You don't know the first thing about me, Sam."

"Sure I do."

She shook her head no.

"Then tell me," he said.

"My apartment isn't far from here. It's just a studio. But I keep it neat. Maybe you could walk me home?"

"OK," he said. "But first, tell me what it is you think you don't want to tell me." A drinking problem, a divorce, a married lover, an abortion, an abandoned child? It was all tame news to him. "You'll feel better."

"No, I won't feel better."

"Where did you go after you quit the agency?" he asked. "What did you do?"

"In those days, I thought you underestimated me."

"I've always thought the world of you, Evie."

"You never knew who I was, Sam."

"Sure I did."

"You still don't. When I read your book about the Falcon . . . the parts about 'Effie,' about me."

"That book's fiction," he said.

"Hardly."

"I never meant to hurt you, Evie."

"Don't make me feel pathetic."

He didn't know what to say, so he put his arms around her.

She tried to talk but was interrupted by tears.

He pulled her closer, pressing his lips against her ear, feeling the silkiness of her bobbed hair. When her body shivered in a sob, he felt a wave of desire for her. With his fingertips he turned her face to his, putting his lips against her skin, kissing her salty eyes. Distraught, she was more attractive to him than she'd ever been before. Tears made him want her in ways her youth and good humor never had. He chose not to consider what this suggested of him—he knew better than to believe it was compassion. Instead, he kissed her and she kissed him back. Her lips were soft, her mouth warm.

"Take me home," she said.

He waved down a cab.

"I've always loved you, Sam," she announced a moment later in the back seat. By then he was beyond weighing her words with care.

In her apartment, there had been few words.

Now it was morning and he suspected he'd made a mistake.

"Sam?" she said, as he slipped out from under her.

"Shhh," he said.

She smiled and rolled over, still asleep. She'd had a lot to drink the night before.

He dressed in silence, looking around the studio apartment, which he'd seen before only by moonlight. The furnishings were sparse—a desk, a wooden chair, a battered armoire, a worn love seat. On one wall hung a calendar that had been a promotional gift from a local dairy and featured for each month a different picture of farm scenes; for this month, Evie had crossed out with an *X* all the days leading up to yesterday, which hadn't ended yet for her. On another wall hung a cheap print of a painting of the Hudson River School. No photographs of family. No books. Little to suggest a personal life. He turned to the desk near the window and opened the top drawer; inside were a few pencils, note cards, paper clips, and a dog-eared copy of *The Maltese Falcon*, which he removed. He glanced at Evie, then turned back to the light and flipped through the book, stopping at the underlined passages, all of which featured Effie Perine. Evie had circled one line of dialogue—Spade tells Effie she is "a damned good man, sister." In the book's margin, Evie had scribbled: "He can go straight to hell." Hammett knew Spade had intended it as a compliment.

Still, he couldn't blame Evie for misunderstanding.

He glanced to check that she was still sleeping, then took a pencil from the drawer and quietly moved to the love seat, settling with the book open on his lap. He was the author of the goddamn book and so if anybody was entitled to clarify one of the character's motives it was him. He'd write a few new lines of dialogue, crossing out the old. Later, Evie would find the book tucked under a pillow, peruse it, discover his handwritten revisions and be reassured that Sam Spade had only ever harbored affection for his secretary Effie Perrine, just as Hammett's feelings had always been warm toward Evie. Why not reassure the kid? Christ, he and Evie were never cut out to be serious lovers. (This despite the evidential, disheveled condition of the bed across the room, where Evie lay in a contented heap.) They were always just good friends, or something like it—nothing wrong with that. But he also wanted her to know that she meant more to him than the starlets he picked up with regularity (and sometimes with Lily's begrudging knowledge) in Hollywood. And by revising just a few lines of dialogue, he'd make Evie understand all this, and, in the meantime, spare himself the need to talk, talk, talk it all through. He had a train to catch.

He settled back and perused the pages of his famous novel.

After a moment, he closed the book, allowing the pencil to roll off the arm of the loveseat and onto the rug.

No go.

He didn't know how to make the damn thing clearer. Sure, he could change "good man" to "good girl" and take out the "sister" business altogether, but that wouldn't accomplish much. Not when he suspected that what Evie really wanted was to be seen as something of a siren, a femme fatale, a dangerous woman. But none of these things played for her; on the page or in life, such a description would read only as ironic. The last thing he wanted was to seem to be making fun of her. And all of this was beside the point, anyway. There was a larger problem. It had taken Hammett only a moment to realize that he couldn't just call up the narrative voice he'd employed when he wrote the book. New dialogue between Sam and Effie? He might as well have tried to come up with something new for Oedipus and Jocasta to discuss, in ancient Greek. Time passes. He was some other kind of writer now.

No matter.

It had been a vain, foolish idea anyway—what would Evie have cared about his scribbling after he was gone?

He stood and moved quietly back across the room, returning the book to the drawer and then taking his wristwatch from the nightstand. It was almost 8:20. His train left at 9:40 from the Third and Townsend Street Station, which was at least fifteen minutes away. He still needed to stop by his hotel to pick up his suitcase and check out. Of course, he couldn't just leave her. He'd dress and then wake her.

He slipped into his trousers.

Afterwards, he looked for his shoes but one was missing. He got onto his hands and knees and looked under the bed.

There, he found the second shoe.

And something else as well—a rosewood tray, half the size of a desk blotter, which he slid with great care from under the bed and into the light to examine. On the tray was a small wooden box, a spirit lamp, a bamboo pipe, a sponge, a needle, a spoon, and a pair of small scissors for the lamp wick. He'd seen dozens of similar opium layouts in Chinatown. "Jesus," he whispered. It explained a lot about the way she was living and why she'd been so evasive about herself the night before. He opened the small box. Inside was the hypodermic needle.

He looked at Evie.

He knew how it worked with junkies—even good-hearted ones. His old character, the Continental Op, had helped a beautiful girl get off the stuff in *The Dain Curse*. But that was fiction. And Hammett wasn't much like that character anymore—broke and lonely. Now his life was good. Books, fame, money, Lily. Besides, you could never trust an addict to give you a straight story. And he was no Dr. Freud. He hadn't the time for this.

Maybe he needn't wake her after all.

He slid the tray and opium kit back under the bed.

Climbing to his feet, he carried his shoes across the room, placing them on a lace doily atop Evie's dresser, between a tulip-shaped bottle of perfume and a foot-high statue of the Virgin Mary. From his pocket, he removed a small notebook, tearing out a page with slow, precise attention to make no sound. With the stub of a pencil, he wrote "San Francisco General Hospital, Dr. Peter Gelker," and set the note beside the perfume. From his wallet, he took three C-notes, folded them in half, and set them beside the note. Sure, he knew the cash was as likely to be used to buy more stuff for Evie to put into her arm as it was to pay for the treatment at S. F. General. But the choice wasn't his. She'd decide. She was too damn old to treat like a child (particularly when he barely had time for his real daughters, Mary and Josephine, whom he resolved now to visit as soon as he got back to Los Angeles, to give them each a hug and bring them something nice).

What a mess the morning had become.

Now, he just wanted it to be over.

With shoes in hand, he crept toward the door. He would put the shoes on after he latched the lock behind him and was outside on the landing that led down to the street. But as he opened the door, he heard the bed creak. He turned to see Evie leaning up onto one elbow.

"Sam, are you going?"

Her hair was twisted about her head.

"I wanted to let you sleep, Evie. I have a train to catch. I'll telephone you."

"I don't have a telephone," she said, squinting in the light that streamed through the Venetian blinds. "It's funny that a perceptive guy like you wouldn't have noticed that."

Actually, he hadn't. "We'll get together next time I'm in town."

"I woke up just as you were dropping money on my dresser."

Damn, he thought.

"Money, Sam, like I'm some kind of whore?" she continued. "Tell me you didn't do that. Tell me I dreamed it. Please."

Three hundred bucks was a hell of a lot more than even the best whores got for a single night, he thought, though he knew better than to share that observation just now. "Look, I was just . . ." He stopped. He'd be damned if he'd talk about why he left her the money, damned if he'd allow his providing her with the financial means to get out of trouble become the impetus for a conversation that would pull him right into it. No, it was better she find the note with the money after he cleared out. She'd figure his motives then. "I've got to go. I'll drop you a line from LA."

One moment more and he'd have been out the door . . .

"Sam, there's something I want to tell you."

He stopped, his hand on the knob.

Her voice sounded oddly flat as she asked: "Do you still have that stone Falcon, the one from the case all those years ago?"

"What?" This was the last thing he expected.

She pulled herself to a sitting position, wrapping the sheet around her bare shoulders. "A man came here a while back. He said he'd give me money if I'd help him get the statuette. But I didn't take his money, Sam. I didn't tell him you had the thing. Do you know why?"

"Who was this man?"

"I didn't tell him because I can't be bought," she said, ignoring Hammett's question and answering her own.

Those with opium kits hidden beneath their beds usually had a price, and it tended to be cheaper than others, he thought. Maybe Evie was different. He'd not test her by threatening to take back the cash. "Let's not get caught up in that, Evie. Just tell me who the man was."

"I didn't get his name."

"Why'd he want the thing?"

She shook her head hard, as if clearing it. "That's not the point of my story, Sam."

"Why'd he want it?" he pressed, his voice edging toward anger.

She waved off his question, but answered it nonetheless. "He said there was never any fake Falcon, that the black rock was the real thing. He called it a *cintamani*."

"A what?"

"I remember the word because it sounded like 'cinnamon.'" She ran her fingers through her disheveled hair. "I don't know what it means. Something to do with Hinduism or Buddhism."

He'd look it up later. "And you'd never seen this guy before?"

"You're missing the point."

Hammett wondered if the man might have been Moira O'Shea's old friend, the professor from the mental institution. Had the poor bastard been deceived by Moira into believing that Hammett, rather than Moira herself, still possessed the bird? It would be like her to pull such a switch. But hadn't their story revolved around Grail mythology? This must be someone else, similarly deluded. Hammett stopped. What did any of it matter to him in the real world?

"I don't have the thing anymore," he said. "I gave it away."

"I don't care whether you have it or not." She turned away. "I was just giving you a heads-up, just doing you a favor before you left."

"Thanks."

"And I wanted you to know I didn't take his money," she continued, turning back to him. "I could have, but that's not what I am."

He looked at her. "I know that, Evie." He realized then that he'd likely never see her again. This was their curtain scene—she, disheveled and hung over, he, anxious and distracted. He took her in with his eyes. She was no saint, no goddess of sincerity, despite initial appearances. He didn't want to speculate as to how she made money to sustain her habit (no mention of office work or any other kind of job the night before). Maybe that explained her sensitivity to the cash on the dresser. Maybe that's where all the men left their money. No matter, he still thought she was worth the whole damn bunch of starlets back in Hollywood. And he still hadn't space for her in his life. And he never would. "Listen, I have a train to catch." He turned for the door.

"But Sam . . ."

He kept going, making the train south with barely five minutes to spare.

TIME MAGAZINE

DECEMBER 4, 1939
CARL SANDBURG

Hammett settles himself on a bench in Central Park. From here, he can make out the shuttered boathouse and the frozen lake and, beyond, the tall apartments that line the avenue all the way up to Morningside Heights. In the gray light, the stone buildings look like so many grave markers. Meantime, all around him, the park's barren trees are skeletal monuments. Hammett is not uncomfortable here in his wool hat, coat, and muffler. The townhouse he shares these days with Lily is overheated, which she likes but which makes him feel sluggish. He needs air, cold, solitude. Didn't his first real writing take place on a park bench in Union Square back in San Francisco as the fog rolled in over downtown? He can't use the luxurious study Lily has prepared for him. The thick curtains and paneled walls belong in a mortuary. It is no place to work. It is better here, equipped with a yellow legal pad and three pencils sharpened with such expertise that they could be used for eye surgery. He wonders why it's taken him so long to give up the idea of composing on the typewriter. The machine is efficient but lacks lyricism. Pencil and paper! Make a mistake . . . simple erasure! No pressure. As in many things, children set the best example: scrawling pictures with crayons, sculpting with clay, and writing the first drafts of their themes with pencils. Page one of a lined pad is merely page one, not a silent indictment. Don't the Orientals say that a trip of a thou-

sand miles begins with a single step? He jots two words: "The woman."
He stops. Almost everything he's ever written could have begun with
those words, he thinks. Of course, there remains the question of what
comes next. He doesn't know. He rips out the page, folds it in half,
and inserts it in the legal pad, which offers another blank start. A gust
blows through the park. Hammett pulls his coat tighter. The yellow
pages riffle. Meantime, the wind directs a sheet of glossy paper towards
him, a magazine cover (torn from its thick contents). It flutters and
flashes red in its approach, skipping across the barren ground, a sidewalk, around a garbage can, and finally wrapping itself against a nearby
light post, fluttering like a desperate animal in a trap. He sets his writing
pad down on the bench, stands and goes to the glossy sheet. It is the
cover of a *Time* magazine dated a few months before. He folds it along
the crease. On the front is Carl Sandburg, poet of Chicago, the city
of broad shoulders. Hammett hasn't broad shoulders. For that matter,
neither does Baltimore, his hometown. He wonders if Sandburg does.
Who knows? But Hammett knows this much: Sandburg isn't sitting on
a park bench near Lake Michigan freezing his ass waiting for words to
come. No, he is warm and indoors, working. And he can go straight to
hell. Hammett tosses the magazine cover back into the chill wind and
watches it flutter deeper into the park. When he returns to the bench
he discovers that the page he tore from his pad ("The woman . . .") has
slipped from its tucked place and blown away, disappeared. His trio of
pencils has rolled off the bench and into the dirt. And he'll be damned
if the temperature hasn't dropped about ten degrees since he got here.

And if a third character or element lends further credence to the story's "fantastical" elements, then the reader must accept that the story's "reality" is not bound by the limitations of his or her own. It is another world, or a vehicle for capturing a truly "other" aspect of our own world—a wonderment.

—Dashiell Hammett, from an article published in
The Young Writer's Monthly Journal, August 1927

HOLLYWOOD, 1940

Hammett slid out of the backseat of a maroon and black taxicab, unfolding his lanky frame onto the sidewalk outside Musso & Frank's eatery on Hollywood Boulevard. The day was warm, the sky hazy. He straightened his suit jacket and settled his felt hat on his head, breathing deeply. The air smelled of the porterhouse and New York cuts grilling inside. It had been almost twenty-four hours since he last ate. In that time, alcohol had sufficed—now, the scent of steak made him a little hungry, despite the ache in his head and the uneasiness about his gut.

"That'll be two-eighty," the cabbie called to him through the open front window.

He'd order steak and lobster today. The lunch meeting, like the entire trip west, was on the Warner Bros. account and he'd be damned if he'd let Jack Warner off for one cent less than he could stick him for. Of course, food would be the least of the tab, if Huston matched Hammett drink for drink.

"I don't have all day," the cabbie called. "Two-eighty!"

Hammett dug into his trousers pocket. He leaned into the cab and handed the driver a twenty dollar bill.

"I don't have change for that," the driver said.

"Keep it."

"Hey, thanks, Bud. You a millionaire or something?"

Hammett shook his head no. "It's found money."

"Yeah? I wish I could find a little money, just for once in my life," the driver said, pulling away from the curb and into traffic.

"You just did," Hammett observed.

Hammett thought of movie money as "found money." Radio money was the same. What else was an honest man to make of large checks that arrived in the mail for books published years before? It was seven years now since his last novel, *The Thin Man*—too damn long to have accomplished only false starts, dead-ends, or nothing at all. Still, the checks found their way into his mailbox. And now *The Maltese Falcon* was being filmed for the third time, the first two versions having failed miserably. Hammett was here today to discuss the latest adaptation. The director was a first-timer named John Huston, a competent screenwriter who had also worked as a painter and a second division professional boxer and was well-known around Hollywood as a tough-talking, hard-drinking womanizer who, according to Lillian, occasionally demonstrated moments of preening effeminacy that would be just the sort of thing to get under Hammett's skin. But Hammett had nothing to lose meeting Huston. As a novel, *The Maltese Falcon* had sufficient reputation that no movie could damage it. Besides, found money was never a bad idea—if for no other reason than that it meant you could give a little cash to a cabbie or a doorman who wasn't so fortunate as to receive royalties for work they'd done more than a decade before.

"Hello, Mr. Hammett!" the barman called when Hammett stepped into the wood-paneled shadows of Musso & Frank's.

"Hello, Paul," Hammett replied.

"It's good to have you back, Mr. Hammett."

It would be good to be back, if he really were back.

"What'll it be?" Paul asked.

The steaks here were good, but not as good as at John's Grill in San Francisco. Nor were the burgers as good as at Twenty-One in Manhattan. But food was not Hammett's principal consideration when it came to a bar and grill. He liked this place because Paul poured the most generous drinks. "You got any of the twelve-year-old stuff?" he asked.

Paul turned away, selecting a bottle. He poured the drink.

Hammett took the glass and drank. "I'm meeting John Huston," he said, setting the glass back on the bar. "You know him? He's a screenwriter."

"Sure, he's all right."

"Yeah?"

"Sometimes."

"And other times?"

"Asshole," Paul said.

"Sometimes good guy, sometimes asshole," Hammett mused. "That pretty much describes everyone, doesn't it?"

Paul nodded. "What distinguishes one guy from another is the percentage, good guy to asshole."

"And what's Huston's percentage?"

"Seventy–thirty."

"Which way?"

Paul laughed. "I'll let you find that out for yourself."

"Thanks."

"Your regular booth?" Paul asked.

"We'll need a little more light than usual." There were no windows in the place and Hammett ordinarily occupied a corner booth, the dimmest, where he liked to bring his "chippies"—voluptuous starlets or creamy-skinned studio secretaries who were drawn to a tall, handsome novelist whose actual past included the same hard-boiled detective work that made his books compelling. In the dim light, they'd share a few drinks, followed by a little fondling. Sometimes they'd leave together. Sometimes they'd part with barely a kiss on the sidewalk. It didn't matter much either way to Hammett. Of course, Lillian disapproved of his affairs. She had vengeful affairs of her own, Hammett knew. But he didn't care—at least not enough to alter his own ways.

"We can put you over near the big lamp."

"That'll do fine," Hammett said. "How's your family these days, Paul?"

"Good. And yours?"

Hammett's ex-wife and two daughters lived in Los Angeles, though he didn't always call on them when he came into town. "Jo's fourteen now. Mary's almost ten," he said to Paul. He sent monthly checks, birthday cards, and Christmas presents, sometimes phoning from New York to inquire after the girls' schoolwork or playground friends. But he never knew how to talk to little girls. How would he know? Sure it was a shame, but life was full of shame if you went looking for it. He thought most times it was better for everyone when he just slipped in and out of California.

"They grow up fast," Paul said.

Hammett loved his girls. Sometimes he missed them. His ex-wife never pressed him and the girls didn't know any different. Perhaps if he were another kind of man. . . . But what could come of speculation like that except a waste of whatever identity one actually possessed. "Pour me another, Paul."

He settled into the booth, his back to the wall so he would see Huston before Huston saw him—an old habit from his PI days. Five minutes later, when the young director walked into the grill, Hammett had one unobserved moment to look him up and down. Huston was nearly as tall and thin as Hammett himself, with a striking, hangdog face that was not handsome but that no doubt appealed to some of the same Hollywood starlets who kept company with Hammett in the dark booth across the room. His step was light—was this the effeminacy that Lillian had referred to, or was it a characteristic Huston had developed dodging jabs in the ring?

Huston squinted, adjusting to the dimness.

"Over here!" Hammett called.

Huston spotted Hammett, then he grinned with the confidence that only a proper combination of youth, wealth, and talent can provide. Hammett did not grin back; he himself was no longer young, his own wealth was dependent on screen and radio adaptations of old work and his talent. . . . Once, he'd believed "talent" did not exist—that it was a manifestation of mere intelligence and hard work—but the slump that dogged him now suggested otherwise. He reached for his drink and took a slug.

Huston ambled toward Hammett. "There he is!" he called from across the room, putting everyone in the place as much on notice to his own arrival as to the presence of Hammett. "America's greatest writer of detective fiction. Goddamn!"

Hammett stood to greet the younger man.

"I'm honored to meet you," Huston said as he offered his hand.

"Pleasure's mine."

"Can I call you Dash?"

Hammett nodded. He liked "Dashiell" for book jackets. In life, he preferred Sam. But Lily called him "Dash," and now all of Hollywood and New York knew him by the name.

"I had the pleasure of meeting Lillian a few weeks ago at a party," Huston said, settling opposite Hammett. "She talked so much about you that I feel we're already acquainted."

"Yes, she's a great talker," Hammett said.

"Good writer, too."

Lily's plays had made her nearly as famous now as Hammett. He had suggested to her the premise of her first, *The Children's Hour,* shortly after they began their on-again-off-again living arrangement and had since offered criticism of every play she'd written. But he never confused the source of her work's quality, which was Lily herself.

"She's a jewel, Dash."

Hammett wondered if Huston was attracted to Lillian. She was no looker, in the ordinary sense. She was like a lump of coal, he thought, which only at its compressed heart contained a jewel of surpassing beauty. He knew she would not be flattered by the image (what woman would?) but he thought it accurate. He wondered if she'd been attracted to Huston. Perhaps that was why she'd told Hammett she found Huston effeminate. A diversionary tactic.

A cocktail waitress arrived to take their orders.

"Ask Paul to keep the good stuff coming our way," Hammett said, handing her his empty glass.

She went away.

"Adapting your work is the opportunity of a lifetime, Dash."

Enough ass kissing, Hammett thought. He'd put a quick stop to it. "There's something familiar about all this, John."

"What do you mean?"

"Déjà vu."

"Oh?"

"Yeah. See, you're not the first director I've had this conversation with, in this very restaurant, regarding this same material." He recalled Del Ruth, who in '31 had described to Hammett his ambitious intentions for *The Maltese Falcon*'s first screen adaptation. "Very promising words at the time, but it didn't come off well in the end."

Huston said nothing, but inhaled deeply.

"This isn't even the second time a director has sat across from me in this very booth and told me he thought 'The Falcon' was first rate," Hammett continued, recalling the second version, which the studio released as *Satan Met a Lady*. "Would you call that déjà vu, John? Or something else?"

"Something else," Huston answered without hesitation.

"Yes, what?"

The first-time director considered his response. "I suppose if a man's around long enough, everything starts to feel familiar to him."

Hammett laughed. Huston might be worth a damn.

"I saw both of the earlier films," Huston continued. "Train wrecks, absent the fascination."

"Glad to hear you think so," Hammett said.

"Don't worry, Dash. We've obviously got a damn good story. And a damn good cast."

Damn good director? Hammett wondered. "Did you get George Raft for the lead?"

"He turned it down. It's his loss."

"So who's playing Spade?"

"Humphrey Bogart."

Hammett sat back. Bogart had only played second leads, usually a "heavy." Was Warner cutting his stake, transforming the project into a "B-picture"?

"You don't like him, Dash?"

"I like him all right, but . . ."

"But what?"

"Look, in the book Spade's morals are ambivalent. He's no knight in shining armor. But he's not a flat out crook, either."

"Bogart can play more than just crooks."

Hammett said nothing.

"He's got a lot of screen charm that hasn't been tapped yet," Huston continued. "Believe me, you'll see. He's going to be an A-list star after this one. Don't worry."

He didn't like being told not to worry, as if he were an old woman. "I don't worry about movies, John."

There was that damned grin again. "I shouldn't be surprised to get a 'hard-boiled' response from the inventor of the genre."

"I didn't invent anything."

"You're too modest. But that's all right, we'll make a good team." Huston leaned back in his chair. "See, I have no problems with modesty."

"Give it time."

"We'll see."

Hammett couldn't help wondering if he could still take the younger man, despite Huston's reputation as a boxer. Once, Hammett would have finished the fight before any "boxing" got started. No Marquis of Queensbury shit. Instead, a knee to the groin, then the blackjack—Pinkerton maneuvers. But Hammett was forty-five years old and most days he felt sixty-five; he didn't know anymore if he could fight his way out of a paper bag.

"What are you working on these days?" Huston asked.

"A new book." At least, he'd like to be working on a new book.

"How's it coming?"

Not at all, Hammett thought. Not even a single page. "Very well," he said.

"Does it have a title?"

Hammett had no desire to discuss writing. "How'd you convince Warner to let you make a third run at the Falcon, John?"

"I showed him the new script."

The script had been delivered by courier that morning to Hammett's suite.

"Read it yet?" Huston asked.

"It's damn good."

Huston slapped his palm on the table. "You just made my day!"

"Why wouldn't I like it, John? It reads like I wrote 90 percent of it."

"You did. But the figure's more like 95 percent."

The drinks arrived.

Huston drew nearer the table and lowered his voice. "Warner insisted on seeing a script before he'd give me the go-ahead. So I asked my secretary to take your novel and re-type it in standard script form.

I intended to work off it as a first draft. But somehow her typescript wound up on Warner's desk without my ever seeing it. An overzealous mail boy must have picked it up. I was furious. Until, that is, I got the note from Warner telling me it was one of the best scripts he'd ever read."

Hammett shook his head. "You ought to share screen credit with your secretary."

Huston laughed. "Sorry, union rules."

Hammett drank.

"Of course, I made a few minor changes," Huston said.

"I noticed."

Huston waited.

Hammett let him wait.

"Well?" Huston pressed. "What did you think?"

A waitress arrived with menus, which she handed to Hammett and Huston. Her hair was netted so tightly into a bun that it pulled back the corners of her dark eyes. Her uniform was spotless. "I recommend the clam chowder," she said.

"Manhattan or New England?" Huston asked.

She smiled. "Oh, I'm from Bakersfield, but people peg me for an Easterner all the time. I think it's something about my manners."

Hammett and Huston looked at each other.

"I meant the clam chowder," Huston said, turning back to her.

"Oh, that's made here. Locally. In the kitchen."

Hammett laughed. "How long have you been working here, dear?"

"This is my second day."

"We'd never have guessed you were new," Huston observed.

"Thanks," she said.

"I think Gracie Allen stole your act," Hammett said.

She looked confused. "No, she's older than me. If anything, it'd be me who stole her act, except that I don't have an act."

"Ah, right," Hammett said.

"Do you two know Gracie Allen personally?"

They shook their heads no.

"Do you two work in the movies or radio?"

Again, they shook their heads no.

"Oh well," she said. "There're your menus." She turned and started back to the kitchen.

Huston laughed. "Now I'm going to have to order the damn chowder."

"It'd be a shame not to."

They opened their menus.

"Well?" Huston said.

"Yeah, I'll have the chowder too," Hammett answered.

"I mean the script."

"I thought your changes worked, John."

"Excellent."

"The Fat Man lives at the end?" Hammett asked.

"I had a soft spot for the guy."

"I guess that's good."

Huston wiped his lips with his cloth napkin. "I'm flying out a stage actor to play the part. On Broadway, he's had some supporting, butler-type roles, but he can do more than that. Trust me, the camera will love him. His name's Sydney Greenstreet and he's got that oozing, insidious charm you write about. Comical, but you sure as hell wouldn't want to know too much about what's likely a perverse private life. In short, the perfect Gutman. The audience is going to eat it up. You think he needs to buy it at the end, as in the book?"

Hammett knew Huston was going to do whatever he damn well pleased. "Doesn't matter."

"I'll consider it."

"And I noticed you cut a character or two."

"The Fat Man's daughter,"[3] Huston volunteered. "I wanted to streamline that last section of the film."

Hammett drank. "Streamlining's good."

"Actually, I was wondering about her."

"Yeah?"

Huston waved his big hands in the air. "Frankly, Dash, I can't help wondering why she's in the book at all. I mean, she's only got that one scene with Spade in the Fat Man's suite. And when the book's over she's the only character unaccounted for. Otherwise, it's all so tight."

Hammett looked at the younger man. It was true what Huston had said about himself, about his lacking modesty. "You forget, John, that there's one other left unaccounted for at the end. The most important."

Huston narrowed his eyes, confused.

"The Falcon," Hammett said.

Huston nodded.

"Look, it's been a long time since I wrote the book," Hammett acknowledged. "Hell if I remember what I was thinking when I put the girl in."

"I was just curious."

Hammett took a drink. "The 'real' Fat Man, who was known in the rackets as the 'Big Man,' didn't have a daughter," he said. "I invented that character. But you're right. I didn't do much with her. In the end, she just serves as a temptation to dangle in front of Spade. A drugged, half-naked teenager alone in a hotel room, used for years in just that way to distract her father's rivals. Ugly stuff. But I saw plenty of that kind of thing."

"Spade acts honorably with her," Huston observed.

Hammett shrugged. "He's only 70 percent monster."

Huston scratched his long chin. "Maybe I ought to leave it in."

Hammett shook his head no. "Your instincts are good, John. Who knows what I was doing?"

"You know," Huston said.

Hammett didn't want to reveal how little he really knew about his own writing, beginning these days with how to get one word onto the page.

"But other than the Fat Man's daughter, all the other characters were real?" Huston asked.

"Except Spade. He was a composite of private dicks I'd known."

"He wasn't based on you?"

"No."

Huston smirked.

Hammett shook his head, unwilling to waste time enumerating the differences between his fictional counterpart and himself.

The waitress returned. "May I take your lunch orders, gentlemen?" Neither had looked at the menu.

"Can you give us a couple more minutes?" Hammett asked.

"What'll you two have?" she responded, oblivious.

"Just another couple minutes," Hammett repeated.

"You're not even ready to order an appetizer?" she asked, incredulous.

"Chowder," they answered, in unison.

"Excellent choice."

When she was gone, Huston turned to Hammett. "What became of those characters?"

"From '22? Most were killed. Like in the book."

"But the others?"

"Emil Madrid is still in jail."

"The 'Joel Cairo' character?"

Hammett sighed. "One's real, one's fiction. Keep that straight, John."

"And the redhead?"

"Moira." He looked away. "She's still around, somewhere."

Huston drank the last of his scotch and signaled for the cocktail waitress to come back to their booth. The lunch crowd was picking up. "So how'd things actually wrap up with the jeweled Falcon, Dash?"

"Look, why don't you just focus on the story you're being paid to shoot?"

"But the actual jeweled Falcon's still out there, right? Unaccounted for."

"You're getting that look in your eye, John."

"What look?"

"I saw it plenty when I was working this case. It's avarice."

"You never went after it yourself?"

"I'm no thief."

"I'm not talking about it as loot. But as adventure."

Hammett laughed. "I'm not Hemingway, for God's sake. *He* might be willing to get himself killed over a statuette, provided *Life* magazine was reporting his every move, but I have no such aspirations. I saw up close what going after that jeweled bird costs."

Huston finished his whiskey. "Why don't we go after it together?"

Hammett was taken aback.

"I'm serious," Huston continued. "First, we'll shoot the movie. We'll get it in the can. It shouldn't take more than a few months, editing included. Don't worry, I'll do a hell of a job. No question about that. And then we'll make travel arrangements. You and me."

"The trail's been cold for almost twenty years."

"That's all right. I've never been to Constantinople."

"Look, John, it's unlikely the statuette is still there. Hell, there may never even have been any jeweled bird."

"Never?"

Hammett shrugged. "Might have all been a kind of hoax."

The waitress arrived.

"I'm afraid I've got some bad news, gentlemen."

"Out of chowder?" Hammett asked her.

She looked astonished. "How did you know?"

"He's a detective," Huston answered.

"Yeah? A private eye?"

Huston nodded.

"Like Sam Spade?" she asked.

"Not *like* Spade," Huston said. "He *is* Spade."

"The real one?"

Hammett shook his head. "There is no real one, dear. He's fiction."

She laughed. "You're pulling my leg. Of course there's a real one."

By the time Hammett and Huston left Musso & Frank's they were well liquored up, though neither man showed it. Lunch had been good. And they liked each other all right. Now, they walked half a block along Hollywood Boulevard and turned on Highland to the parking lot where Huston had left his new Cadillac, which was as black and shiny as the best shoe leather.

"I gave up driving years ago," Hammett said. "Can't say I miss it."

"Guess you wouldn't." Huston folded his long body in behind the steering wheel. He turned the key and the Cadillac thundered to life. "At least, not so long as the studio boys keep sending limousines for you."

"Is that how you think it is?"

"That's how it ought to be, Dash." Huston palmed the steering wheel through two or three revolutions, like a ship's pilot, to pull a hard right out of the lot and onto Hollywood Boulevard. The car swayed on its suspension. He stepped on the gas.

"Did you get Geraldine Fitzgerald?" Hammett asked. He thought she'd be perfect for the part of Brigid.

"No, she passed," Huston said.

The boulevard outside Grauman's Chinese Theatre was crowded with tourists who thought movies were actually made on this street.

"We signed Mary Astor," Huston continued. "Good break for us. She's made for the role."

Hammett wasn't so sure, but what did he really know about making movies?

Huston turned north onto Laurel Canyon Drive, smoking a cigar and describing his plans for the shoot as he negotiated the twists through the Hollywood Hills and down into the San Fernando Valley.

Hammett listened. Huston pressed harder on the accelerator when they reached the long, flat road that led through orange groves and bean fields toward the iconic 130-foot tall Warner Bros. water tower, which was visible at the foot of the Verdugo Mountains even from miles away. Hammett settled back in his seat. He liked inland Southern California. The dry air was good for his lungs. And sometimes it smelled like oranges. Meantime, Huston kept talking.

At the gate to the studio, a guard waved them through.

Huston steered past the two-story, wooden writers' bungalows where half a dozen or more of Hammett's drinking buddies labored for exorbitant salaries on rewrites of rewrites of rewrites that would likely never get made into movies. It was a crazy business. Next, Huston drove past a city block that resembled a New York street, another block that looked like a European village, and another that was freshly decorated for an old fashioned Fourth of July celebration, in March. Huston pulled the car into a reserved space just outside sound stage 3, where most of the movie would be shot.

Climbing out of the car, Huston opened his arms wide. "Don't you love it here, Dash? The world's largest playpen. Toys everywhere!"

Hammett had taken in about half of what Huston had said the past half hour about camera placement and lighting. But it was enough to encourage him that Huston might make something decent out of his book. The lot was chaotic and loud, as always—movie extras in period costumes, trucks delivering flats and furniture, teamsters shouting, executives striding with eyes set steadfastly either on the ground before them or on the pages of whatever script they were skimming as they moved from one meeting to the next. And starlets in an ever replenishing supply. Hammett watched a particularly appealing pair pass. "Yeah, lots of pretty toys here," he observed.

Huston grinned.

Hammett thought it might be a good idea to stop at the commissary before leaving today. There, he'd make the acquaintance of one or another costumed Marie Antoinette–style courtesan or leather-clad Indian princess or other fleshy female fantasy made real by the studio's costume, hair, and make-up departments. He was still a famous man, and courtesans and Indian princesses liked that.

"This way," Huston called.

Hammett followed him through the metal door of the sound stage, which closed behind them with a heavy thud. Inside, the dim, airy silence was almost sepulchral.

"Franklin!" Huston called into the expanse. "Are you here?"

"Mr. Huston?" responded an echoing voice.

"Give us some light, Franklin."

Somewhere, switches were thrown and the vast interior was illuminated.

"Come this way, Dash."

The sets were almost complete. Spade's office, Spade's apartment, the Fat Man's suite, Brigid's apartment, the DA's office, a hotel lobby, a few exteriors. The stage was not lit for shooting, so shadows crossed everywhere. Viewed from behind, the sets were mere slapdash carpentry—from the front, worlds.

"This way, Dash," Huston said.

Hammett followed him onto the set of Spade's office, which featured two desks, a hat stand, office chairs, and a false window upon which was painted in reversed letters, SPADE AND ARCHER.

"What do you think?" Huston asked.

Hammett liked the leather swivel chair behind Spade's desk. He sat in it. In his gumshoe days, Hammett had made do with a plain wooden chair. But he did not begrudge his fictional Sam Spade a little more luxury. "Quite comfortable," he said.

"Too comfortable?" Huston asked. "You think it's out of place?"

Hammett shook his head no. On the desk before him was a clever gadget that dispensed lighted matches. "Where'd you get this?"

"Tijuana."

"I like it." Hammett fumbled with a sack of Bull Durham tobacco set on the desktop beside a pile of cigarette papers. The prop people were good. He looked around, imagining what Spade would see sitting in this spot. Through the false window was a painted flat of San Francisco, featuring the distant Golden Gate Bridge and a working neon sign that alternately spelled "DRINK" and "KLVW."

"We've brought the story to the present," Huston said.

"Sure, why not?" Hammett stood and walked across an empty space to the next set, Spade's apartment.

"You like the framed photographs?" Huston asked, pointing over the mantelpiece.

Race horses. "Your ponies?" Hammett asked.

Huston nodded.

"Spade would approve." Hammett picked up one of the books that lay scattered about the room. He read the spine, "Duke's *Celebrated Criminal Cases of America*."

"You mention it in the novel," Huston offered.

Hammett put it back. "You've done your homework, John." He crossed another open space to the set of the Gutman suite, which was as luxurious as the Spade apartment was spartan. Oriental lamps, silk flowers in cut glass vases. He sat on a striped, satin loveseat. "Almost as decadent as my suite at the Beverly Wilshire."

"I've modeled all the decadent characters on you and Lily."

Hammett laughed. He rose and walked to the set for the O'Shaughnessy apartment; there, a prop master had set the Maltese Falcon sculpture on the mantel of the fireplace.

"That doesn't belong there," Huston said.

Hammett picked up the black bird. "It's got to be some place."

"Yeah, but not just any place."

Hammett looked at the sculpture. "The real one was smaller. Obsidian."

"You mean the counterfeit, from '22?"

"Yeah, but it wasn't so detailed. It was more primitive."

"We can change it."

"No. This'll do."

"Maybe we could use the real one," Huston suggested, brightening.

"The stone counterfeit?"

"Sure."

"I don't have it," Hammett said.

"Who does?"

Hammett shrugged as if he didn't know. He didn't want to explain.

"Too bad," Huston observed.

"It's just a rock, John. Except . . ." He stopped.

"What, Dash?"

"Well, I heard some tales about the counterfeit's 'true nature.' Crazy stuff having to do with mystical powers."

"Your book refers to knights and medieval intrigue."

Hammett set the sculpture back on the mantel. "These yarns were crazier, if you can believe such a thing is possible."

"Try me."

Hammett thought he'd best be careful how he approached this. Huston liked a yarn as much as the next guy, but his critical skills were honed sharper than most. Hammett would leave out Moira's Holy Grail nonsense. "You ever hear the Sanskrit word, *cintamani*?"

Huston narrowed his eyes for a moment and then shook his head no.

Hammett glanced into the dark corners of the sound stage as if he were only half interested by his own words. "In both Buddhist and Hindu mythologies, a *cintamani* is a mystical stone that grants the mind its 'proper attainment.'"

Huston shook his head. "Sounds like Sax Rohmer stuff. Ripe for a B-movie."

Hammett put his hands in his pockets. He turned back to Huston. "You're right John, but . . ."

"But what?"

"Well," Hammett said, "the difference between something seeming real or coming off as false is always in the telling, not the tale itself."

"What are you getting at here, Dash?"

"John, do you believe an object can be charmed?"

"Like a rabbit's foot?"

"Something like that."

Huston grinned and removed an inch-long carving from his pocket. "This is a called a *munachi*. It's soapstone carved by the Quechua people, who live in the Andes."

He handed it to Hammett, who turned it over in his palm.

The image was of two flat-headed lovers facing one another, kissing and joined in erotic embrace. "Pre-Columbian?"

Huston nodded. "It's a charm used to enact sexual love spells."

"And you walk around with this?"

Huston nodded. "The charm was given to me a few years ago by a raven-haired beauty attached to the Peruvian embassy who I met in Mexico at a diplomatic reception. On a moonlit terrace, she suggested the gift would be as much for her own pleasure as for mine. I'm not one to tell tales, Dash, but judging from what occurred afterwards in my hotel room, the munachi works. The Peruvian beauty and I went our separate ways. But I keep the charm with me always. Together, this little stone and I have seen much distinguished action." Huston snatched the stone from Hammett's palm and slipped it back into his trousers pocket. "Sorry, but my wife would never forgive me if I lost this little fellow. Nor would any of the others."

Hammett nodded.

"Do *you* believe in charms, Dash?"

Hammett considered.

"Is this about the Falcon?" Huston pressed. "The actual story? Is that what you're getting at? Was there something about that counterfeit bird, the rock?"

Hammett shook his head no—he sure as hell wasn't going to share with the younger man the fullness of his encroaching foolishness. "The Falcon's just the stuff dreams are made of," he answered.

"Hey, that's good," Huston said, taking a small notebook from his jacket pocket. "Maybe a curtain line for the movie."

"What's wrong with the way the book ends?"

"Nothing, but . . ." Huston picked up a pen from Spade's desk. "As the screenwriter, I'm obliged to come up with at least a few lines of dialogue that aren't already in the book."

"I guess Shakespeare won't sue you for plagiarism."

Huston brushed aside the comment. "The day we have to give that guy the credit he's due is the day we're all out of business."

Hammett clapped Huston on both shoulders. "Your sets are excellent, John. Bogart and Astor will be a fine pair. You're going to do a good job, and the movie's going to work."

"If there's anything you think can be improved . . ."

"Nah, let's get out of here."

They returned outside to the Cadillac.

"You want to go someplace to get a drink?" Huston asked.

"What do you say we swing by the commissary?" Hammett said. "Buy drinks for an Indian princess or two."

"OK, but I'm not letting you borrow the charm, Dash."

"Fortunately, John, there are some things I can still do without hoodoo."

"*Some* things?" Huston asked, intrigued. He fixed Hammett with a hard look. "And some things you can't?"

The bastard was too smart for his own good, Hammett thought. "Just a joke . . ."

"Ah."

"Look, on second thought let's call it a day, John. I'm tired."

Huston looked at him. "You sure?"

Hammett gestured toward the writers' building. "There's a couple guys I've got to catch up with in there," he said, holding out his hand for Huston to shake. "You go on. I'll catch a ride from somebody or other later."

Huston looked confused. "You sore at me, Dash?"

"No, I'm impressed as hell."

Huston shook his hand. "Yeah?"

"Yeah, John."

Huston smiled. "If you're impressed now, just wait till you see the finished film."

Hammett patted the younger man on his shoulder.

"Adios," Huston said.

Hammett watched the long, black Cadillac pull out. He turned, but didn't walk toward the writers' building. Instead, he made his way back to soundstage 3.

"Franklin, can we have the lights again?" he called into the darkness.

A metallic thud preceded the illumination.

Hammett crossed the empty front half of the cavernous building, his footsteps echoing, to Sam Spade's office set. He stopped in the place Huston had told him a camera would be placed. The set indeed looked a lot like the office he'd shared in '22 with his old partner, Mike Arnette. He turned and glanced around the silent sound stage. No sign of the mysterious and powerful Franklin, giver of light, no sign of anyone. Hammett stepped onto the set and, after a moment, took a seat in Sam Spade's chair. He leaned back, putting his feet up on the desk as he used to do at the end of long days. Everything had seemed possible back then, even if so little that was good had yet come to pass. He closed his eyes and breathed deeply and for a moment allowed himself the fantasy that when he opened his eyes he'd be back at his desk in San Francisco, 1922—broke, over-worked, unhappily married, but full of possibility.

The voice came from out of the darkness. "Sir?"

Hammett opened his eyes, looking around. "Who's there?" He took his feet off the desk.

A tall, thin colored man emerged from the shadows. "Oh, I thought for a moment you were Mr. Huston," he said.

Hammett shook his head no. "Are you Franklin?"

"Yes sir. Watching over this sound stage is my responsibility."

"I see."

"Are you one of the actors in Mr. Huston's movie?" Franklin asked.

TIME MAGAZINE

NOVEMBER 10, 1941
RITA HAYWORTH

Hammett sits at his desk, his hands folded atop the keys of his typewriter, his mind wandering; the world is going to hell, and Murrow's nightly broadcasts from London make Hammett wish he could personally do something to stop the goddamn Nazis. Unfortunately, he is neither a politician nor a military strategist nor a trans-Atlantic industrialist; nonetheless, he knows that as long as his country remains on the sidelines, the best a man can do to prepare for the eventual entry into war is to continue doing his regular job efficiently and selflessly. For now, factory workers need to keep working hard in their factories, farmers keep farming, engineers keep engineering, builders keep building. And there lies the rub. What, exactly, is Hammett's job these days, besides going to the bank to cash checks that arrive from film and radio adaptations? Is he a writer anymore? Lily writes, that's for sure. Her new play, packing houses on Broadway, works well both as a family drama and as a political allegory about Fascism in our midst. President Roosevelt sent her a note, for God's sake! Of course, Hammett knows better than to believe the only kind of writing that matters is that which expresses an obvious political or social message. He knows there aren't good kinds of writing or bad kinds of writing, there is only good writing or bad writing. And what is the first, essential characteristic of good writing? That it exists. The sheet of paper currently rolled into Hammett's typewriter is blank. Not a noun, not a verb, not a goddamned article. Hammett is indolent just when what his country needs most is working men. No sense denying it. He takes a deep breath and looks away—enough useless and only half-rational pondering for now. He pivots away from his typewriter and reaches for a magazine set beside his uneaten lunch on the coffee table. Rita Hayworth is on the cover. What a fine piece of ass. Auburn hair, his favorite. She's as good a looker as his old flame and nemesis, Moira—probably better if you actually put the two women side by side. Yes, the world is going to hell, but Rita's long, perfect legs make a man grateful for small mercies. Nonetheless, after a moment, he puts the magazine down. Wherever the world is heading, he's already in hell, he thinks. After all, where else would a man fail to be distracted from his troubles even by Rita Hayworth? The cover photograph may as well be of Rin Tin Tin for all the good it does him. He turns back to the desk and pulls the blank paper from his typewriter, placing it to the left of the machine atop a quarter inch high stack of other blank pages, all likewise pulled in the past few hours; from a taller stack to the right of his typewriter he takes a new sheet and rolls it into the machine, staring at it as if he might find something already typed on it in the faintest ink.

Readers will stay with you provided your characters remain plausible even in "implausible" circumstances. Surely, the potion in Stevenson's Dr. Jekyll and Mr. Hyde *is make-believe; nonetheless, many readers respond with as much suspense to the gas-lit, fantastical tale as they do to more realistic material because Stevenson's* characters *seem real.*

—Dashiell Hammett, from an article published in
The Young Writer's Monthly Journal, August 1927

WESTCHESTER COUNTY, NEW YORK, 1942

Hammett crushed his cigarette in the ash tray beside the plate of sliced tomatoes and the jar of pickles that Lily had set on the kitchen table to impress their guest, film producer Hal Wallis, with how folksy their life was here at their newly purchased, rustic getaway. The maid had laid out a platter of sliced roast turkey, cold cuts, and a stack of sliced, freshly baked bread. A country lunch. Earlier, Lily had mixed mint juleps, fancifully describing her New Orleans upbringing as she poured tall glasses for Hammett and Wallis, whose soft-spoken manner belied the confidence and sharp intelligence that made him Jack Warner's right-hand man. He was here today to discuss the film adaptation of Lily's latest play, "Watch on the Rhine," which Warner Bros. had bought for a hundred and fifty grand. Wallis was good at his job—his last picture had been *Casablanca*. Still, this notion of his that Hammett should write the screen adaptation for Lily's play . . .

Hammett wasn't sold.

"Can you pass the pickles?" Wallis asked as he slathered mustard on a slice of bread.

Lily obliged, smiling.

Hammett was glad she was happy here at Hardscrabble Farm. She deserved it, the clever witch. Only an hour and a half outside Manhattan, the 150-acre property was a world away from the big town. Meadows, woodlands, stables, bridle paths, guest houses, a caretaker's house, and this beautiful, white clapboard main house. A dusty, two-lane road ran past the house and neighbors regularly stopped by with freshly baked pies or newly bottled cider or other practical, tasty offerings of country sociability. In return, Hammett would offer expertly mixed cocktails. His room on the second floor overlooked a spring-fed, eight-acre lake that was surrounded by dogwoods. These past weeks he had spent many hours sitting at his desk watching the light change on the water below. He studied the deepening shades of green, orange, yellow, and blue. Too bad he wasn't Monet, he thought, who could have made something of it. Some evenings, Lily and he put their feet up in the living room and listened to radio programs. It all made for a pretty picture. But the nights were actually quite long and his sleep was not good here.

"Bette Davis wants to do it?" Lily asked.

Wallis nodded. "Provided we pump up her part, make it a lead."

Lily shrugged. "Bette *is* a lead."

"What do you think, Dash?" Wallis asked.

"Who says no to Bette Davis?"

"So we're all agreed," Lily announced, cheerfully.

"You grow these tomatoes here on your farm?" Wallis asked her, spearing a slice with his fork and dropping it onto the pad of lettuce and pile of sliced roast turkey already balanced on one of his two slices of rye bread.

She shook her head no. "Next season."

Hammett affectionately put his hand on her hip. "Who'd have guessed that a Jewish girl from New Orleans whose entire adult life has been spent in Hollywood and Manhattan would be a milkmaid at heart?"

"Moo," she said.

"That's great, so long as you don't stop writing," Wallis said to her.

"Oh, that'll never happen," she said, cheerfully.

Never was a long time, Hammett thought. Still, he didn't doubt her. She had no troubles at the typewriter, however neurotic she might be in other circumstances.

"You a farmer these days too, Dash?" Wallis asked.

Hammett preferred the stables and woods to tilled fields, though he didn't mind getting his hands dirty on occasion. And he found some of the scientific literature on horticulture fascinating. "I'm more a farmer in theory than in practice."

"Kind of like your writing these days, eh Dash?" Wallis asked, folding his slices of bread together and setting the completed sandwich on his china plate.

Hammett looked at him.

"Onions!" Lily said, slapping her palm on the kitchen table hard enough to make the platter of sandwich fixings rattle. "I forgot to slice onions." She turned away. "What's a sandwich without onions?"

Hammett shot her a glare. "Forget the onions. Hal asked me a good question."

She stopped. "Obviously, he's kidding, Dash."

"Why is that obvious?"

"Because of course you're writing."

Over the years, Hammett had told her at least half a dozen ideas for new novels—but did Lily actually believe that was writing?

"Look, I'm just playing around, Dash," Wallis said.

Hammett took a long, slow breath, as if gathering his composure. Then he turned, expressionless, to Wallis. After a moment, he broke into a wide grin. "No, Hal, *I'm* just playing around."

Lily laughed, perhaps a little too loud.

"*You* never play around, Hal," Hammett continued, still smiling. "With you, it's work, work, work . . . all the time. But that's why you're the best. Always angling, right?"

"OK," Wallis acknowledged as he scooped a spoonful of potato salad onto his plate. "The truth is I did come here today to convince you to write the screenplay, Dash."

"With a new, star part for Bette."

Wallis nodded. "Of course you'll also have to open up the story." He turned to Lily. "I mean, a single, interior setting is practical on stage, but it's deadly for a film, naturally."

"Naturally," Lily said.

Hammett wasn't hungry, but he put a dill pickle on his plate just to be sociable. "Let Lily adapt it. You know damn well she can."

"Of course she can," he answered. "But the studio prefers to bring in a second perspective."

"That's a good idea," she said.

Hammett took a noisy bite of the pickle.

"Look, Dash, the army's loss is going to be the studio's gain," Wallis said.

Surprised, Hammett looked at Lily, then turned back to Wallis. "You heard about that?"

The producer nodded. "But this is going to be an inspiring, patriotic film. See, there are plenty of ways to fight the fascist bastards. Still, I'm damn proud of you. A man your age . . ."

"My age had nothing to do with it," Hammett said.

"Sure, but still . . ."

Hammett stopped him with a wave of his hand.

A few days before, Hammett had gone to the army recruiting office in New York City, volunteering to enter as a forty-five-year-old private. He'd told no one his plan. Lily was furious when she learned what he'd done. Her anger was assuaged, however, when he told her they'd classified him 4F. His ticker and lungs had passed their tests (despite the pulmonary trouble he'd had since his brush with tuberculosis as a teenager during the last world war). Of course, a bad heart or lungs would have allowed him a measure of dignity. No such luck. The army turned him down because he had bad teeth.

"You told him?" he asked Lily.

She shrugged. "I mentioned on the phone how much I admired your courage."

Hammett laughed. "You called me a selfish bastard when I told you I'd tried to enlist."

"As I said, Dash, there're lots of ways to fight the Nazis," Hal said, trying to ease the tension.

Hammett turned to him. "Such as 'opening up' Lily's play for the screen, right?"

"Actually, yes."

Hammett set the pickle back on his otherwise empty plate. "OK, we open with the family on a train." He made a wide-screen gesture with his hands, "They're chug-chug-chugging through the picturesque Mexican desert toward the American border, all talking excitedly about their new prospects, the children thrilled to see their mother's Yankee homeland for the first time. German husband, American wife, kids with Teutonic accents, Mexican desert."

Wallis smiled, admiringly. "It's visual, exotic, and unexpected in a film about Nazis in New England. See, that's what we want from you, Dash."

"And what I just did . . . that's war work?" Hammett didn't wait for an answer. "Let's see, it's the equivalent of how many dead Nazi soldiers?"

"This isn't a joke, Dash," Lily said.

He took a breath. "I know, Lily," he admitted.

"You bring a fresh eye to it," Wallis said to him.

Hammett shook his head. "Talking it is easy, but . . ."

"But what?" Wallis pressed.

Hammett said nothing.

"Just talking it through like this is good," Lily said. "Scene by scene. I can type it up later. Flesh it out. It'll still be your work."

Hammett fixed her with an angry glare. "You're nobody's goddamn secretary, Lily. Least of all mine."

"I just meant . . . ," she started.

"You know damn well that talking isn't writing," he snapped.

"Hell, Dash," Wallis said, setting his plate down. "When it comes to the movies, *writing* isn't writing! It's all just pictures and talking."

Hammett shrugged, unconvinced.

"So will you do it?" Wallis asked him.

Hammett looked around the kitchen. "Say, what happened to our goddamn mint juleps?" He didn't wait for an answer, but turned to Lily. "That is, *your* goddamn mint juleps, Lily."

She put her plate down, wary.

Hammett looked conspiratorially to Wallis. "Let me tell you something, Hal. The mint's julep's a great drink if you're at the Kentucky Derby or if you're Margaret Mitchell talking to Selznick about making *Gone with the Wind*. But don't you think they're a little cloyingly antebellum otherwise?"

"Well, now . . . ," Wallis started.

Hammett interrupted. "Ah, but Lily loves juleps. If there's one thing she loves even more than gabbing on the telephone about subjects she ought to keep to herself, it's stirring her goddamn pitcher of juleps on warm days. But adding sugar to alcohol . . . seems redundant to me. Of course, when it's the only drink offered what are you going to say, eh Hal? It's better than nothing, right? That's why you and I have been sporting juleps today. I've got twenty-year-old scotch whiskey in the cabinet, but here we are pretending we're Ashley Wilkes. Anyway, weren't our sugary drinks here a minute ago? Where the hell is my julep?"

"Maddy took them out to our place settings at the dining room table," Lily answered, her voice hard. "Everything's set."

"What the hell are we eating out there for?" Hammett demanded. "This is sandwiches, not Thanksgiving dinner."

Lily fixed him with a glare of her own. "We have a guest."

Hammett turned to Wallis. "As I recall, don't friends sometimes eat sandwiches together in their kitchens, even in Beverly Hills?"

"Sure."

Hammett pulled a chair out from the kitchen table. "So have a seat, Hal. Let's be country."

Wallis remained standing. "But if Lily's already set the table . . ." He stopped.

Hammett nodded, suddenly calm. "You're right, Hal." He turned to Lily. "My apologies, dear. I can offer as an excuse for my brutishness only my sudden, embittered state of julep-lessness."

She looked at him. "Don't give me any of that Nick Charles crap."

"You're so right, Nora," he said.

She looked away.

He scooped a spoonful of potato salad onto his plate. "Let's eat," he said, starting into the dining room. "And there'll be no talk of business while we're *formally* dining!"

Later, Wallis returned to the city without a commitment from Hammett.

Lily retreated to her room.

Hammett couldn't take the quiet in the house so he went for a walk.

❖

The late afternoon sun was bright and cold.

Sometimes, walking the property reminded Hammett of his boyhood wanderings through the marshlands of Chesapeake Bay, liberated for short periods from the racket and mechanized stink of Baltimore. In those days, the experience was vast, energizing, and awe-inspiring. He'd felt a stranger in a strange land, capable of marvels. This afternoon's walk was good too, but different. Tramping the fields now, he was reminded by the fetid earthiness of the alfalfa, livestock, and manure that, like them, he too was possessed of an actual, organic existence—a walking compost heap. It reassured him to know that were he to fall dead in the fertile bracken he would provide actual food for countless organisms, both micro- and macroscopic, and in this way, at least, be connected to the world. It was dark when he returned to the house.

All the lights were on. Good, he thought. Lily wasn't sulking.

Not so good, however, was that a Rolls Royce limousine idled at the end of the driveway, the silhouette of a driver visible in the half-light, another larger shadow discernible in the back seat. Naturally, Hammett assumed Wallis had come back to resume his sales pitch about writing the script. *Hollywood generosity* . . . a seeming oxymoron that troubled Hammett now because Wallis's good intentions might actually be real. Hammett was far more comfortable with studio executives farming out work either to hacks or to egomaniacal geniuses like Huston than their allowing personal considerations, like jump-starting some blocked bastard's writing career, to inform their decisions. He'd be damned if he'd be anybody's charity case. Hammett strode up to the limousine, resolved to invite Wallis in for a belt of the twenty-year-old scotch and then to send him home with a firm "no" to his proposal, rather than with the weak, postponed answer with which they'd parted earlier in the day.

The backseat window rolled down. But it wasn't Wallis's face.

"Ah, Mr. Hammett, my old friend."

Hammett pulled back, resisting an impulse to jerk away from the window. Involuntarily, he shook his head. "Gaspereaux?"

The Big Man chuckled, his jowls quivering. "I do admire a man who's unafraid to display his shock so nakedly upon his countenance. Some might find such an expression comical, but I find it heartwarming when it comes from an old comrade in arms."

Comrade? They'd never been on the same side. "I thought you were dead," he said, trying to will his heartbeat back to a rhythm of mere panic rather than borderline coronary.

Gaspereaux took a long, rattling breath and grinned. "Isn't it a marvel, my old friend, when one's thoughts prove to be inaccurate? Oh, it may be momentarily disconcerting, but ultimately it's liberating. Preconceptions are such dull gatekeepers, don't you find? Only a fool resists the delight of contradiction, eh? And you are no fool, my dear sir. You are surely wise enough to recognize a situation such as this as a gateway to possibilities previously unimagined. Marvelous, marvelous."

This was impossible. Hammett had seen Gaspereaux gunned down on the street. He'd attended the funeral. But nobody else talked like this . . . In Huston's movie, Sydney Greenstreet had reproduced the rhythm and intonation, but even he had come up short of capturing the full decadence of the Big Man's actual tone. (Government censors would likely never have allowed such a portrayal anyway.) But here it was again—the real thing.

The driver, a short man dressed in an ill-fitting black suit and with the build and mug of a boxer, climbed out.

Hammett stepped away from the car.

The driver nodded obsequiously as he moved around to the passenger side, where he opened the backseat door and indicated with an awkward sweep of his paw for Hammett to climb in. "Please, sir."

Hammett didn't move.

"Come, my old friend," Gaspereaux rejoined from inside, sliding to make room in the backseat. "Won't you accompany me for a little ride? Surely you can spare a few minutes."

Hammett said nothing.

Gaspereaux leaned back toward the open door, flipping on a soft, rose-colored overhead light to illuminate the back seat. "Naturally, I'd be delighted to get out and join you in your lovely home to meet your celebrated paramour," he said. "I am an admiring consumer of her Broadway products. However, I believe it will behoove you and me to conduct our 'catching-up' in private."

Hammett didn't want him inside the house. He looked around. All was quiet, dark. He'd never outrun the driver, so he leaned forward, looking into the wide back seat. "It's been a long time since I was a gumshoe, Gaspereaux. But as I recall, taking rides with gangsters is something to avoid."

Gaspereaux looked stricken. "My friend, you can't possibly believe I mean you harm!"

Hammett said nothing, but noted that the pug-faced driver hadn't budged from beside him.

The folds around the Big Man's eyes narrowed. "Nor, my cautious comrade, can I deny being struck to the quick to learn that you still think of me as nothing more than a . . . what did you call me, a 'gangster'?"

Hammett wondered if by chance Lily might glance out her window and notice him out here. Unlikely . . . And even if she did, why would she find anything unsettling about his talking with someone unseen in the back of a limousine? Like Hammett, she'd assume it was Wallis. There would be no phone call to the sheriff—who was miles away regardless. Hammett was armed only with his house key and a penlight. (Since when did a man have to arm himself for a stroll around Westchester County?)

"You misjudge me, my friend," Gaspereaux reassured him, his voice rumbling wet in his lungs. "I have changed. All that you once knew of me, well . . ." He blew on his fat fingers and gestured as if gently releasing a butterfly to the breeze.

From old case notes, Hammett knew this:

Cletus Gaspereaux, aka the Big Man, had been born in England in the 1870s and for the first three decades of his life moved among a crowd of Dickensian "underworld" types whose diverse and profitable business enterprises spanned London. His inventive mind proved useful not only in East End alleys, but also in the private boxes at Ascot, where horse races proved little more difficult to fix than dice games down on the Thames. When Scotland Yard drove him from London he fled to New York City with a trunk-full of cash and appetites large enough to consume the world (food, Cuban cigars, and adolescent boys). For years, he lived in a cosmopolitan whirl, driven not only by "mix-ups" with local police or mob bosses, but also by his relentless pursuit of the statuette known as the Black Falcon, which culminated in 1922, San Francisco. Hammett had brought the curtain down on the Big Man's plot, resulting in Gaspereaux's "fatal" shooting by one of his own henchmen. Hammett had seen it with his own eyes. However, considering present circumstances, he wondered just what he'd actually seen and how much he'd ever actually known.

"What the hell," he said, folding his long body to slide into the backseat. Both fight and flight were out of the question. And this was at least shaping up to be something other than a boring evening. "What's the worst you can do to me, Gaspereaux?"

The driver closed the door after him.

"Kill you, I suppose," the Big Man answered, smiling. "But why ever would I want to do that, my old friend?"

"Oh, everybody's got their reasons," Hammett said, settling back into the cushy leather. His sense of resignation calmed him. The Big Man and his thug were either going to shoot him or they weren't. He preferred one outcome over the other, but either was all right in the end. He watched the driver pass around the front of the car and climb into his place behind the wheel. "You've got this backseat lit like a whorehouse, Gaspereaux."

The Big Man chuckled. "I am impressed with how quickly you've regained your composure, Mr. Hammett. I do hope you are at least a little impressed with me as well for having caused you to lose it in the first place, even if only momentarily."

The driver pulled away from the curb. Where to? Hammett would be damned if he'd ask. "Yeah, I'm impressed, Gaspereaux. It's that 'back from the dead' business that really grabs a guy's attention."

"Allow me to assure you, my old friend, that I am no ghost. Would you prefer I turn out the 'whorehouse' light, Mr. Hammett? Darkness is no unwelcome stranger to me."

"No, that's all right."

"As you wish," Gaspereaux said. "You're my guest."

The limousine audibly kicked up gravel as it skidded and then accelerated on the dark, country road.

"You're looking very distinguished these days, Mr. Hammett," Gaspereaux said, straightening the wrinkles of his trousers as he burrowed deeper into his roomy corner of the backseat. "The lines on your face have finally caught up with that prematurely white shock of hair. Yes, you're looking sufficiently world-weary to be of interest to a sculptor or portraitist. You're a bit too thin, of course. But then, my perspective adjudges 99 percent of the population as being underweight, ha ha . . ."

"Yes, you're still looking well-fed," Hammett answered.

"I have never believed in self-denial." He took a deep, raspy breath and then straightened as if inspired by a new thought. "My dear Mr. Hammett, while we're on this subject, I must admit to having been somewhat disappointed with your choice of moniker for me in your famous, fictionalized adventure story. I'm the 'fat' man? Naturally, my vanity cares not a whit about being described as 'fat.' How can I deny its accuracy? But as a student of literature . . ." He chuckled and rubbed his puffy hands together. "The rhetorical advantage of the adjective 'big,' as it's used in my *actual* street moniker, as compared with the unsatisfactory 'fat' as used in your story, is that 'big' refers not only to my girth, but also to my status *and* to my capacity for the visionary."

Hammett leaned toward the Big Man. "You've waited how many years to object to one word?"

"I comment only as one of your devoted fans, dear sir."

Hammett nodded. "Well, the associations with 'big' are indeed as you describe them. However, I chose 'fat' because of that word's associations with decadence, greed, and revulsion. As such, I still believe I chose the right word. But then, we're not here to talk about literature, right Gaspereaux?"

"Call me Cletus."

Hammett glanced out the window, but could see only his own rose-colored reflection and nothing of the dark country passing outside. "Look, what do you want with me, Gaspereaux?"

The Big Man clapped. "How refreshing to be with a man who lets you know exactly where he stands! The world is so overfull of prevaricators. I've always admired your directness, Mr. Hammett. Even in our San Francisco adventures. There is much to be said for having friends who are straight shooters, don't you think?"

"Speaking of straight shooting," he replied.

"Yes, I was shot," Gaspereaux interrupted. "Your eyes did not deceive you, my friend. I can show you the scars here under my garments if you wish."

Hammett shook his head no. "Keep your finery buttoned."

"As Mark Twain, your literary predecessor in the pantheon, once said to a reporter, 'rumors of my death were greatly exaggerated,'" Gaspereaux continued.

"I didn't know lard could stop lead."

Gaspereaux laughed. "Be assured, my friend, the surgeons performed wonders at the hospital." His tone turned confiding. "Gads, they had to sew up this organ and that organ. Lucky me. Nonetheless, upon awakening I still faced the criminal charges with which you'd saddled me and all the subsequent indignities to which flesh is heir when it is relegated to your barbarian penal system, if you know what I mean, my dear sir."

"You bribed the doctors?"

"And the Coroner's office, the mortuary, a police lieutenant, and two journalists who mistook the writing of obituaries for actual news reporting."

Hammett couldn't help admiring Gaspereaux's instinct for survival, though he'd never admit it aloud. "And then you disappeared?"

"Yes, but not aimlessly. Indeed, my departure from this lovely country was no mere retreat, but an offensive."

"Everything you do is offensive."

Gaspereaux chuckled. "Ah, I do so admire a man with a rapier quick wit. But getting back to my point . . . You see, I never gave up on our little adventure. No, I traveled from San Francisco back to Constantinople to confront the Russian, still determined to acquire that which I'd been cheated of."

"The jeweled statuette?"

"Yes."

Judging from the limousine, Hammett wondered if Gaspereaux had indeed recovered it. "And?"

"The Russian was gone from Constantinople. It took me fifteen years to track him down."

Hammett waited.

"At last I found him in his garret on the Left Bank in Paris."

"How romantic," Hammett sneered.

Gaspereaux shook his head. "The place was squalid. And the pathetic wretch was dead, sodden in a cot that reeked of his own blood and urine. His heart had stopped just hours before my arrival. Natural causes, of all things! It pained me. Oh, what fragile beings we are, my dear sir. Surely, you understand human frailty better than most, being the compassionate man of letters you have shown yourself to be in your thrilling works of literature."

"So he didn't have any jeweled bird?" Hammett inquired.

The Big Man chuckled. "Come now, my friend. Would I have found him alone in a garret if he had? By now you must know the truth—there never was a jeweled bird."

Hammett said nothing.

Gaspereaux pulled himself out of his cushy corner and slid nearer his guest on the back seat. "Of course, seeing as I only learned all this myself after decades of searching for a jeweled bird . . . Perhaps, this truly *is* coming to you as news, my good man."

"And that news?" Hammett pressed.

"The real bird has nothing to do with jewels."

Hammett sighed and brushed away the words. "Yeah, I heard an old wives' tale once."

"Was it Egyptian?"

Hammett shook his head no. "It was pure foolishness."

The Big Man chuckled, clapping his hands like a grotesque infant. "However foolish the tale you were told may have seemed to you, my good sir, *you* remain the greater exemplar of foolishness! But please take no offense. You are not alone in this. I too once possessed the actual treasure, only to angrily toss it off as worthless. Surely, you and I share the distinction of being the biggest fools in the world!"

Hammett indicated the limousine in which they were riding—not an ordinary conveyance for a fool. "You seem to have done all right for yourself, Gaspereaux."

The Big Man leaned forward and lowered his voice. "In the interest of disclosure, sir, I must admit that this lovely car is merely 'borrowed' and that its owner may not yet have discovered that fact. But shed no tears for him. He's the sort of Wall Street type that I deduce from your left-wing politics you disdain. Besides, he'll get the car back from the police impound after we abandon it tomorrow or the next day. And until then . . . well, a man such as myself has to get around in style."

"Nothing changes."

"Ah, there you're wrong, sir." He slapped one fat palm on Hammett's thigh while with his other hand he reached into his coat pocket and removed a wooden jewel box the size of a silver dollar. "Things are changing even as we speak. Yes, I am quite confident that soon I will own my own *fleet* of limousines, seeing as I have recently acquired the small item in this box."

"Which is?"

The Big Man grinned, pulling the jewel box away. "Allow me to explain, my dear sir."

Hammett waited.

"In ancient Egypt," Gaspereaux began, "certain stone statues were believed to contain the spirits of deities. Understand, sir, I am not speaking figuratively. The stones actually contained the gods. These objects were known as 'ka' stones. They had *power*, and . . ."

"The counterfeit statuette," Hammett interrupted. "You're going to tell me it was no counterfeit, right?"

Gaspereaux narrowed his eyes. "Moira told you?"

"In '33. Sans the Egyptian angle."

The Big Man grunted. "Well, since my sources indicate you've been absent of the statuette lo these long years, I assume she absconded with the thing?"

"I gave it to her."

The Big Man's eyes widened.

"Small enough price to get her out of my life," Hammett said.

Gaspereaux burst into laughter. "You couldn't be more wrong, sir! You'd have been better off giving her one of your eyes."

Hammett said nothing.

"The rock you once possessed is of Egyptian origin."

Hammett shook his head, doubtfully. "She said something about Arthurian myth. And there's an Oriental angle, too."

"She was misinformed, my good sir."

"To say the least."

The Big Man ignored his skepticism. "You may recall from your schooling, or perhaps from your eclectic, autodidactic reading, that the Egyptian god Horus, known as the god of kings, manifested on Earth in the form of a . . ." He stopped, waiting like a school teacher for Hammett to answer.

Hammett would be damned if he'd say it.

"Yes, a falcon," Gaspereaux said. "Naturally, the ka stone in which the spirit of Horus was contained was the most powerful of all. Over the centuries, it has remained powerful, never decaying like the pyramids or the Sphinx. Today, it is still able to provide power, wealth, or the fulfillment of any desire to its owner."

"Did Moira feed you this line?"

"No, I've neither seen nor heard from that dear girl since '22, when I was still in the dark about this. Doubtless, she thinks I'm dead. But I've looked for her. Wouldn't I love to surprise her as I surprised you tonight? And then to take from her the actual bird. But as you may already have discovered, she seems to have disappeared from the face of the Earth."

Hammett had made a few inquiries of his own and likewise had come up with nothing about Moira's location. "So if the Russian was dead when you found him, who told you the yarn?" he asked.

"Someone quite unknown to you. Someone now deceased." He sighed and shook his head, ruefully. "Ah, the terrible, violent ends some unfortunates derive for themselves."

Who? Hammett wondered. And how? But there were some questions better left alone. "What's in the jewel box?"

Gaspereaux opened the box to display a shaving of black stone hardly larger than a fingernail. "It's a piece of the black bird, the stone statuette you once possessed."

Hammett laughed.

"How dare you laugh at me!" Gaspereaux exploded, unable to

conceal his anger. "You *gave the bird away* to Moira, who has disappeared with the treasure!" He stopped, taking a long, rasping breath to calm himself. The effect seemed immediate. "Forgive my outburst, dear sir." He rubbed his pallid face with his hands. "I am a passionate man," he continued. "And I adjudge you to be passionate as well. This doubtless allows us to understand each other as men of the world, true?"

Considering the circumstances, Hammett thought it unwise to further annoy his car mate. "True."

"So allow me to explain."

"Go ahead."

"I learned from my now-deceased contact that a small piece of the bird had been chipped off near its right eye," Gaspereaux said, a barely restrained enthusiasm crossing his face. "I had a new goal! If I could not find the bird, due to your foolishness, I might yet find the chip. And this is that chip, my foolish friend, acquired at great expense, both financial and mortal."

Hammett shook his head. "What do you want from me?"

"Surely not your approval," Gaspereaux said, snapping shut the jewel box and returning it to his coat pocket. "I am not foolish enough to believe you could ever find it in your fragile ego to offer approval. After all, that would require you to admit to yourself what a fool you've been. No, all I want is to ask you one simple, direct question, sir."

"What do you want to know?"

"My memory is imperfect, but you, an author, able to have recreated our little San Francisco adventure with such accuracy . . . Tell me, sir, was the bird statuette you possessed indeed chipped near the right eye?"

Hammett laughed. "Christ, how would I know? You think I studied the ghastly thing? It was a paperweight to me, nothing more."

"Think, man!" Gaspereaux demanded. "Surely you gazed upon it for many hours during the years it was set upon your desk. Close your eyes, man, revisit the scene. Use that celebrated mind of yours for something other than pulp fiction, damn it!"

Hammett did his best, though he wasn't going to close his eyes. "It was worn down, like it had been left in a stream for a long time. A chip here or there . . . who knows? Who cares?"

"I care, sir."

Suddenly, an image of the bird actually came into Hammett's minds' eye. Gaspereaux was right—Hammett *had* stared at the statuette over the years while he conceived one or another line of dialogue for his detectives, criminals, and *femmes fatales*. Now, he recalled aspects of the bird's face—particularly, how alert the thing looked, despite the crudeness of its design. But the details of its ancient stone surface eluded him. A chip here or there? Oddly, he recalled the thing as being pristine, though that was impossible. No matter. He knew Gaspereaux would never settle for uncertainty. And Hammett would be damned if he'd offer him false satisfaction. "You've been cheated."

"You lie!" Gaspereaux snorted. "Stop the car, Franco," he called to the front seat.

The driver swerved to the side of the road, skidding to a stop on the shoulder.

"Get out," Gaspereaux said as he reached up and switched off the overhead, rose-colored light

Now, Hammett could see outside. All was darkness. "Here?"

"Yes, here," Gaspereaux instructed.

It was the middle of nowhere, but Hammett knew better than to argue. He climbed out and closed the door after himself.

The limousine sped away, its taillights fading to nothing.

After a moment, the dust from the tires settled and the woods came to life—cicadas, an owl, the sound of a stream someplace nearby. Soon, even the blackness gave way to shades of gray and silvery highlights. It all suddenly felt so dreamlike that for a moment Hammett wondered if Gaspereaux and his stolen limousine had ever actually been there.

But how else could Hammett have wound up here, miles from home?

He turned and started walking.

❖

It was nearly midnight when he opened the front door to the house. Surprisingly, the lights in the entry were still on. Lily ordinarily made a show of turning off all the lights whenever he returned home unaccountably late (quite often); the darkness would leave him to stumble and muddle through the house. Poor woman—he knew he was no prize. Not anymore. Not by a long shot. But he still didn't understand how his breaking his neck by eventually tripping over an umbrella or forgotten parcel in the darkened entry would set things right. No matter. Tonight, she'd left the lights burning. Perhaps she'd fallen asleep before she got to the light switches to inflict her feeble protest, he thought. But she wasn't asleep.

"Dash?" she called from upstairs.

"Yes, I'm home."

She appeared at the landing, still dressed as she had been that afternoon, and then flew down the stairs toward him, waving a sheaf of pages.

"I've been working," she said, stopping at the bottom.

"Oh?"

"Yes, where've you been, Dash?"

He didn't feel like telling her the story. He was tired, having walked six or seven miles. Besides, he doubted she'd believe he'd been kidnapped by Cletus Gaspereaux, who'd come back from the dead in a Rolls Royce limousine to inquire about a small chip from a sacred stone. Hell, he wouldn't believe it himself if he hadn't been there. Doubtless, she'd already concluded he'd met some local woman with whom he'd spitefully spent the last few hours in bed. Hammett was long past explaining himself—all that was left for him to do in his relationship with Lily was to try to not break his neck one of these nights creeping through the entryway in the darkness. "What are those papers you've got there, Lily?"

"The opening scene of the script," she said, glowingly.

"What?"

She showed him the cover page. It read,

Watch on the Rhine
A screenplay by Dashiell Hammett
Based on the play by Lillian Hellman

"What the hell?" he said.

"I just typed up your idea. You know, about the family on a train steaming through the Mexican desert. It's a great opening, Dash. Wallis loved it, too."

He leafed through the half dozen pages. Action, dialogue . . . "My idea was just a setting."

She shrugged. "I embellished."

"You did all this tonight?"

She nodded. "We can work together like this, Dash."

"I didn't do shit."

"Sure you did."

He wanted to slap her hard. The impulse was almost over-whelming—wrong in every way. He fought it, not moving a muscle, closing his eyes, and breathing deeply.

"What's wrong, Dash? You want to change a line of dialogue here and there? That's great, go ahead!"

He shook his head no. "I'm tired and going to bed, Lily."

She stepped back. "OK."

He trudged up the stairs.

"We'll talk more tomorrow?" she called up to him.

"Fine," he said, not turning around.

It was not actually the prospect of a fraudulent collaboration with Lily that moved him the next morning to take a 6 a.m. train into New York City to call on the first midtown dentist who would see him without an appointment. There in the examination room, Hammett put two C-notes into the front pocket of the dentist's white smock and told him what he wanted done. "Pull them all," he said, determined not to be turned down again by the US Army recruiting office in Times Square just for having bad teeth. "Yank every last one." No, it wasn't Lily and the script that brought him to this. He had resolved in the night to talk to her about her story, to kick around ideas; if she needed to put his name on the script to keep the adaptation from being farmed out to someone incompetent at the studio then he'd live with it. Did this compromise him? Hell, she'd do a wonderful job. No, what bothered him far more was that he had spent most of the previous night awake in his bed, wondering if his recollection of the old Falcon statuette—chipped or not?—was at all accurate or if it had been altered by images from his long standing, recurrent dream, wherein the sculpted Falcon's face was not only pristine, but alive, its onyx eyes moving and looking everywhere but at him.

TIME MAGAZINE

JULY 19, 1948
HOWARD HUGHES

The new typewriter is promising, an Underwood Champion. It is portable and takes less space on Hammett's desk than his last typewriter, which was an older Royal that proved disappointingly unwieldy; better yet, the Underwood Champion offers much better key stroke action than the Remington Rand that preceded the Royal. And the Champion's portability offers the opportunity to write on trains or even on a cruise ship. (Pencil and pad are good for nothing more creative than grocery lists, he has come to believe.) He keeps the five typewriters that he's bought since his return from the war in the closet, as he wants to be prepared if a particular passage should call for a particular machine. As yet, he's had no occasion to switch machines, as there has been no call for any typewriting. Still, he wouldn't want a moment of inspiration to arrive without the proper equipment. Lily teases him that he's unwittingly become a collector of typewriters or that his attention to their features and flaws is more suited to a newspaper consumer products reporter than a novelist. But surely Picasso would not begin a painting without his brushes being just so. Oh, perhaps when an artist is young he can scribble finished poems of surpassing beauty on the back of a cocktail napkin, but with age process becomes increasingly important. Or so he hopes, as otherwise he has no rational explanation for his block, his state of mind. Only dread superstition (and Moira O'Shea seeming to have disappeared from the face of the Earth). He rolls a sheet of watermarked paper into the carriage and settles into his straight-backed chair. The room is quiet and the conditions for work ought to be ideal. But something's wrong. After a moment, he pushes away from the desk, stands, and moves across the room, looking back at the new typewriter. Then it hits him. He returns, spins the roller to remove the sheet of paper, and looks hard at the name inscribed in gold on the back of the carriage, *Champion*. Suddenly, the word strikes him as ironic. Oh, he might still strut about Manhattan like a man with a knockout punch, but he knows his jaw is glass, his reflexes slowed, and that he is just one blow from being permanently KO'd. Champion? The last thing he needs these days is a typewriter that each time he rolls a sheet of paper into or out of it reminds him of what he is not. No, this isn't going to work. He turns and shuffles through a stack of already-read magazines on his desk, looking for last week's issue of *Time*, the one with Howard Hughes on the cover. Didn't he see an ad inside it for a new Smith Corona?

Remember, young writers: even that paragon of the rational, Sherlock Holmes, once said that "when you have eliminated the impossible, whatever remains, however improbable, must be the truth."

—Dashiell Hammett, from an article published in *The Young Writer's Monthly Journal*, August 1927

NEW YORK CITY, 1948

Hammett had indulged the cocktail hour at the Stork Club with an army buddy who'd been stationed with him in the frozen Aleutian Islands. Hammett's years as an enlisted soldier, even one well past his prime, had proved less stressful for him than being a "blocked" author. But army life was over and tonight he would have to ask some passing student in the lobby of the Jefferson School of Social Sciences for directions to his own classroom, though he'd been teaching in the same room for almost three years. After too many cocktails, classrooms all looked alike. Chalkboard, desks, bare walls. Once, Hammett had wandered the converted office building that housed the school until well past his seven o'clock start time, looking for his class. Of course, he'd been drunker that night than he was now and the hallways had reminded him of a childhood dream in which he wandered twisting passages in a grand mansion and opened countless doors only to find behind each a brick wall. He wasn't sure what Freud would say of such a dream, but he knew the Marxist reading. And so did everyone else at the Jefferson School of Social Sciences, an "open university" for students and faculty of a politically left-wing persuasion. Eventually, Hammett always found his classroom and the twelve to fifteen creative writing students who waited there to discuss their typed-up stories (which could sometimes be as difficult to distinguish from one another as the classrooms, being similarly drab and half-empty and only slightly dirty). Hammett had discovered that mild drunkenness didn't compromise his teaching or critiques as much as it did his navigation. So he made it a regular part of his regimen every third week or so—or whenever an army buddy dropped in to visit New York City.

"Mr. Hammett," a young woman called in the bustling lobby.

He turned. She looked familiar.

"I'm glad I caught you before class," she said, glancing at her wristwatch as if to calculate how close she'd come to missing him. "I wanted to give you this." She handed him a large manila envelope.

He remembered now—her name was Jeanette or Janet or Jane. She was about twenty years old. Too damn young for him. "This is your work?" he asked. The weight and thickness of the envelope suggested about fifteen pages. A single chapter or short story.

"Yes, but I'm afraid I won't be able to stay for class tonight. I'm so sorry. It won't happen again."

"Well, we'll miss you dear."

"I didn't want to be late handing in the assignment."

"Very conscientious."

According to the course catalogue the weekly night class was "devoted to the history of the mystery story, the relationship between the detective story and the general novel, and the possibility of the detective story as a progressive medium in literature." But Hammett hadn't written the course description. In practice, the class focused more on technical aspects of fiction writing, such as pacing and characterization, rather than on the political implications of committing a murder with a revolver as opposed to an automatic. Additionally, Hammett delivered periodic lessons on the darker aspects of "the writing life," which may have been more education than some students bargained for. But no one complained because everyone here was a comrade. Hammett too believed in the social movement and he cared about good writing and most times he shared generously with his students. Why not? He'd be back to writing fiction himself one of these days, he thought. And then he'd take a little time away from the class. All he needed was a few new pages.

"May I ask why you'll be missing class tonight?"

"Tonight's the wake for my father. It's in half an hour."

"What?"

"Yes, he passed away on Sunday. Very sudden."

"And you're here now?"

"I'm afraid the story's not my best work."

He looked at the envelope in his hand.

"I had trouble concentrating the last couple of days," she said.

"You wrote this since your father died?"

"It's just a first draft."

He wished he remembered her name. He put his hand on her shoulder. "Please accept my sympathies."

"That's all right. Everyone struggles with their writing from time to time."

"I meant your father."

"Oh, of course."

He thought of his own daughters, Jo and Mary, who were about this girl's age. He hadn't seen either for a long time. He wrote them letters and sometimes they wrote back, but he couldn't claim to know them—their letters were little more than lists of day-to-day banalities. Of course, what else would they have to say to a man they'd never known? Still, they'd surely skip a class to attend his funeral. Like this girl. But he wouldn't blame them if they didn't.

"You and your father weren't close?" he asked.

"Actually, we were quite close."

"Then what are you doing here? Go."

She didn't move.

"Don't worry about this, dear," he said, indicating the envelope.

"But my father's gone."

"Exactly," he said. "Don't give the manuscript another thought."

"You don't understand, Mr. Hammett. I need something to come back to. Writing is all I have now, it means everything."

"Oh, I see. I'm sorry. I'll give your work a good look and talk to you about it next week."

"Thank you."

He watched her go.

The encounter sobered him and he had no trouble finding his classroom.

Most of his students were in their twenties, but some were older. A few had studied at prestigious universities and now attended the Jefferson School of Social Sciences to make a political statement. But most lived working-class lives that, until now, hadn't allowed for higher education. Traditional "night schools" were vocational, but here the study of ideas and politics and art counted for more than mere job training. Hammett believed equality and education were essential for any progressive vision of the future. But many Americans opposed the idea of such a school as this. And the opposition was growing fast, particularly in Congress. Rumor of an impending "blacklist" in Hollywood and publishing circulated among the New York intelligentsia. Lily worried, too. "Just be careful what you say at that school, Dash," she advised him once—but only once, as his response to her warning had been swift and terrible. Nobody would tell him what he could or could not say. Just as no one would ever tell him what to write. That is, if he were writing.

"You've come with manuscripts tonight?" he asked the class.

They nodded. Somehow, they never had trouble writing. He resented them only sporadically; more often, he wished just one of them might enter his class with real talent to go along with the much more common attributes of enthusiasm, life experience, and productivity. A protégé. Lily was long past that now. What could he teach her? She was now the more successful of the two.

"Who'd like to read first?" he asked.

A hand shot up at the back of the room.

It wasn't one of the students. Sometimes, mystery fans came to the class to meet Hammett or to ask him to sign a book. He always obliged, though he didn't like to devote class time to it. He looked closer at the older man in the back row. "Well, I'll be damned."

"There's no doubt about that, Sam."

It was Mike Arnette, his former partner from the Pinkertons. Big, bald head and powerful shoulders, heavily lidded eyes. It had been a long time. They hadn't parted on the best terms. "What brings the Ghost of Christmas past?"

Mike held up a few typed pages.

The students in the classroom looked at one another.

"You brought a story to read?"

"This is a creative writing class, isn't it?"

Hammett wondered why Mike had chosen such a public forum for their reunion. It worried him. "Well, I'll be damned."

"Yeah Sam, we've already established that."

The class members chuckled and looked at one another.

"You may be wondering about our guest tonight," Hammett said as he settled into a chair beside the desk at the front of the room. He thought it best to handle the situation with a light touch. "One does not expect to see new faces mid-semester. But Mike's is no new face. Not to me, at least. We go back thirty years. And it won't be a 'new' face to any of you either, if you look closely. Note the deep lines around the eyes and mouth and the graying of the beard." He shook his head in mock sympathy. "Ah, the ravages of time."

"Hey, you're no Tyrone Power either," Mike said.

"Never was."

"That's not what the ladies in San Francisco used to say, Sam."

"Class, this is Mike Arnette, my old partner in my Pinkerton days."

Members of the class mumbled greetings and welcome. They knew Hammett's history included time as a private detective. They knew his experiences had provided source material for more than one of his novels. And a student named James, who insisted on never removing his fedora, even indoors, knew more than the others about Hammett's Pinkerton days—more than any student needed to know. He raised his hand.

Hammett pointed to him.

James turned to the back of the room. "Are you the Mike Arnette who served as the model for Miles Archer in *The Maltese Falcon*?"

Mike glanced up to Hammett. "Don't take long, does it?"

Hammett sighed.

"Why don't you ask the author up there?" Mike said to James. "All I know for sure is that I'm the model for Mike Arnette, every day of my life. But as your professor pointed out, I don't look as good as the original anymore. Hey, that's life, right?"

The class turned back toward Hammett.

This Mike Arnette versus Miles Archer business was the source of unpleasantness the last time Hammett saw Mike, which was in Los Angeles in '41, shortly after the Bogart version of the film opened to rave reviews and great box office. At that time, Mike had burst into the Brown Derby, where Hammett was dining with Robert Benchley and Tallulah Bankhead. Mike was drunk and unhappy that the Miles Archer character was killed off in the first reel and that Archer's fictional wife, Iva, was cuckolding him with the hero, Sam Spade. Benchley and Tallulah initially thought Mike's complaints hilarious. But Hammett knew better. Mike was a dangerous guy, and this wasn't the first time the topic had come up. When the book was published in '30, Mike had expressed similar complaints, but Hammett claimed that the initials "MA" were merely coincidental and, more importantly, that no one from the PI world (including criminals) would be likely to read the novel. But with the success of Huston's version, Hammett knew the scene at the Brown Derby could turn bad.

Fortunately, Tallulah realized the seriousness of Mike's protests and came to Hammett's rescue, pretending to be impressed at meeting the model for what she described as one of literature's "most compelling, if only briefly glimpsed, tragic figures." She asked Mike to go out with her to her limousine to drink champagne. The offer calmed him. Now, Hammett looked around the classroom. There was no Tallulah Bankhead to step up to the plate and take one for the team.

He hoped Mike had mellowed.

"You can't make too much of initials," Hammett said to the class. "Hell, Marc Antony's initials are MA, too. And I didn't base Miles Archer on Marc Antony. Or on Maxwell Anderson or Matthew Arnold or . . ." He strained for one more. "Um, Marcus Aurelius."

"But none of them was ever your former partner in the Black Falcon case," James said.

"Look, James, you're indoors. Will you please take your hat off?"

He shook his head no. "It keeps my head warm. Helps me think."

"Maybe it would be better, James, if you didn't think so much."

James looked confused. Mike said nothing, which didn't reassure Hammett.

"Mary Astor's initials are also MA," a woman student said.

"Yeah, and she was in the Huston movie," another said.

Hammett glanced at Mike. The students weren't helping matters. "Listen, class, the truth is that Mike and I didn't work together on the Black Falcon case. You're confusing fiction with fact." Mike had come down with pleurisy the day after Moira O'Shea first entered their office in San Francisco and he had spent the duration of the actual case at home in bed. But when it came time to write the novel . . . pleurisy? A bullet makes for a better opening—after the second draft, the invented murder of Miles Archer served as the catalyst to the whole story.

"Your professor's telling it to you straight," Mike said. "I was actually at home during that case recovering from a bullet wound." He looked at Hammett, daring him to contradict the story. "See, I took one in the chest the week before while foiling a bank robbery."

The students were impressed.

As far as Hammett was concerned, Mike could tell it any way he wanted.

"But hell," Mike said, "I'm not unhappy to be confused once in a while for the Archer character. Why would I be? You're college students. So I'm sure you're all aware that Archer is one of literature's most compelling, if only briefly glimpsed, tragic figures."

Hammett silently thanked Tallulah once more.

"Are you married, Mr. Arnette?" James asked.

"No."

"Were you married at the time you worked for the Pinkertons?"

Hammett wished he had a gun so he could shoot James.

"Yes, young man. But it didn't last."

"Let's not press Mr. Arnette for details of his personal life," Hammett said. "This is not an interrogation room."

"I don't feel pressed," Mike said. "I feel like a guest speaker."

"If I'd known you were coming I'd have planned something special," Hammett said.

"I'll bet you would."

"But tonight the students have brought their own writing to share. To read and discuss."

Mike grinned, holding up his typed pages.

Ordinarily, only registered students participated in class. "Go ahead Mike."

The students settled into listening postures.

"You made something worthwhile out of your experiences as a detective, right Sam? I mean, by writing the books."

Hammett settled in his chair, removing a pen and small note pad from his jacket pocket.

"Well, what I got here isn't finished," Mike continued. "It's actually just notes for a story. Background information. No dialogue or descriptions. It's not even as fleshed out as our old reports for the Pinkertons. But it's a start. I think you'll like it, class. And I know Sam'll find it interesting, seeing as it relates to our real-life experience."

Mike snapped the pages in his hands as if shaking water from them. He grinned at Hammett, then at the students all around him, but he said nothing.

"Go ahead with your reading, Mike," Hammett said from the head of the class. "We're all listening."

The students waited.

Mike cleared his throat. "Here's my offering for tonight, class. Remember, I'm new to the writing game. Let's see, what's written down here?" He squinted to read.

"A long time ago in a distant place there lived a boy whose family came on hard times. The boy wanted to help his family so he sought the advice of a sage who told him to seek what was known as a *corvia-stone*, which magically increased the wealth and honor of whoever possessed it. Naturally, such a stone was not easy to get." He looked up. "Are you all following this, class?"

They nodded.

"OK," he said. "'Now, the only way to get a corvia-stone was to steal eggs out of a falcon's nest on the first day of April, bring the eggs home, boil them, and then return them to the nest. This is what the boy did. Then he hid and watched. When the mother falcon returned and discovered her eggs hard-boiled she made a terrible, troubled racket and then flew off to a secret place to fetch the miraculous corvia-stone, which she then put into her nest. When the stone touched her eggs they became fertile again. Like magic! The falcon was happy. And so was the boy who removed the corvia-stone from the nest, returned to his downtrodden family, and restored their fortune."

The students looked at one another, confused.

"Is that it, Mike?" Hammett asked.

Mike shook his head no.

"Then go ahead and finish," Hammett instructed.

"Sure thing, professor," Mike said, returning his attention to his manuscript. "Now, you may think the boy's problems were over, but they weren't. See, criminals heard about this stone and mistook it for some other jeweled rock and then the boy and his family got their throats slashed like chickens and all hell broke loose for centuries, right up to this present day." He set the typed pages on the desk. "The end."

Hammett said nothing.

"That's my story," Mike said. He looked at Hammett. "I admit I cribbed some of it from material that was given to me by a client. OK, I jotted it all down. But that's what writers do, right Sam? Crib? Steal?" He didn't wait for an answer, but turned to address the class. "So, what do you literary types think?"

After a moment of silence, the überstudent James raised his hand. "Is this a story for children or adults?"

Mike glared at him. "Didn't you hear me say the kid got his throat cut? So how the hell could it be a children's story? What are you teaching these people, Sam?"

Hammett said nothing.

"Is it derived from some sort of folklore?" asked another student.

Mike shrugged. "Scandinavian. Or maybe ancient Roman. I don't remember for sure."

"But that matters," James said. "Setting is important."

"The setting is here and now," Mike answered. "New York City, 1948."

The students looked at each other, confused.

"I think it could use some dialogue," said another student. "That'd flesh it out."

The students agreed.

"I'm looking for deeper characterization," said a matronly woman in slacks and a man's sport jacket. "And details. You know what they say, 'God is in the details.'"

"God's not anywhere in this story," Mike answered. "At least not the god you're thinking of."

"Is there a political aspect to the story?" asked a fourth student.

Mike considered. "I guess you could say the message is to find what you need and keep what you got."

"Yes, capitalism gone mad," said another student.

Hammett did not allow for further discussion. "Interesting yarn, Mike."

The class turned to their professor.

"Like it?" Mike asked him.

"Magical stone? Falcon's nest? Why not some other bird?"

"Falcons are special."

"I'm not sure about your ending, Mike."

"I'm open to suggestions. Especially from you, Sam, since you know more than just about anybody else about these things. And the story's not over. That's why I'm in your class tonight."

Hammett figured as much.

"You can help me finish it, Sam, right?" Mike turned to the students, his Greek chorus. "Don't you think that's fair?"

They nodded.

Mike stood and gathered his papers. "Your suggestions were excellent everyone. I'm afraid I can't stay for the whole class." He turned to Hammett. "We should grab a quick drink tonight. Catch up on old times."

"There's a little place on Sixth called The Village. See you at 10:30."

The class wished Mike well as he departed—as if he was a benevolent old man.

"Now that he's gone you can tell us the truth," James said to Hammett. "Is he Miles Archer?"

Hammett didn't know who Mike Arnette was anymore.

The next student read a story about growing up in the tenements on the Upper West side.

Hammett found it hard to concentrate on the fiction.

Three hours later he found Mike at the bar.

"Artsy crowd in here," Mike said.

The watering hole was dark and smoky, with a long bar along one wall, a row of small wooden booths along the opposite wall, and crowded cocktail tables between. The crush of patrons served, ironically, to isolate, as nobody could inadvertently pick you out from across the room. The place smelled of tobacco, sweat, liquor, and dry rot in the wooden floors. "You want suits, go to the Rainbow Room. Maybe you'll see Ethel Merman there."

"All I want is a few answers, Sam."

"Then this place'll do."

Mike raised his drink. "To the past."

Hammett drank with him.

"You like teaching?"

"I like the students. They're earnest. Their writing's not always so hot. You still a PI?"

"What else am I going to do, write books or teach college courses?" He laughed. "Did you like my little story tonight?"

"Quite a stunt," Hammett said.

"And there's more too," Mike said. "My client's researched it."

"Who's your client?"

"You know I can't say."

"I never took you for a sap."

"I didn't say I believed this mumbo jumbo, just that I have a client who does. And my client's money is something to believe in."

"Well, good for you, Mike." Hammett called to the cocktail waitress to bring them another round.

"Are you writing these days?" Mike asked.

Hammett gave the standard answer: "I'm working on something new." What he was working on was a fence around the vegetable garden at the country house. "But it's not at a place where I can talk about it just yet."

"And you enlisted?"

He shrugged. "Those fascist bastards had to be stopped."

"Jeeze, the army must have been scraping the bottom of the barrel if they took an old bastard like you." He grinned. "And then they go and put you on a godforsaken iceberg . . . Bad luck."

"The Aleutians were all right," Hammett said. "But my being there wasn't luck. The government sent a lot of 'politically questionable' types to places like that."

"You being a Red is pretty funny, Sam."

"Why?"

"Well, considering the strike busting we used to do."

"Those days don't seem too funny to me."

"You were good at it."

Hammett said nothing.

"You ever miss 'Frisco?"

"Sure."

"How 'bout the PI racket?"

"No."

"Too low-class for you these days?"

"'Class' has nothing to do with it."

"The company you keep these days is pretty fancy."

"You saw where I'm teaching. It's not Yale."

"Yeah, that's true. It's strictly for Reds."

"Nothing's strictly for anybody. But OK, there's a political angle. When did you get interested in politics, Mike?"

"Who said I was?"

Hammett didn't want to discuss politics. His views alienated most people. "So what do you want from me?"

"Information. You had the thing."

"The counterfeit Falcon?"

Mike nodded. "Where is it now?"

"I gave it away, years ago."

"To who?"

Hammett didn't like being pumped for answers. "The thing's just a rock."

"I'm not asking for a geological analysis. I want to know who has it."

Since returning from the war, Hammett had made inquiries about Moira O'Shea, but she'd disappeared along with the bird. "I gave it to Moira," he said. "She came to see me in New York back in '33. She'd just got out of stir. I don't know what's become of her."

"Why'd you give it to her?"

Hammett didn't want to go into that. "You got any ideas about her whereabouts? Or what name she might be using these days?"

"No," Mike snapped. "And that works out pretty damn convenient for you, doesn't it, Sam?"

"What do you mean?"

"I mean that you're claiming to have given the Falcon to the one woman who's disappeared off the face of the Earth. Makes me wonder if you're lying to your old partner."

"Why would I do that?"

"Look, we'll buy the thing from you, Sam. We'll give you a good price. You know it's just a 'counterfeit'? And I notice you're not living as high as you once did."

"I told you I don't have it, and I don't know where it is."

"You think you're too good to help me?"

"I'm giving it to you straight."

"You think you're too good to be my pal, Sam?"

"No, just too tired."

"Once, you weren't so damn fancy."

Hammett said nothing. He'd danced this dance before.

Mike shook his head, disapproving. "You aren't exactly clean your-self, Sam. You weren't no angel when it came to our girl, Evie LeFabre."

"What do you know about that?"

"I know how she ended up, that they found her overdosed in '37 or '38 in some dump in Chinatown, right?"

"It's a shame."

"And you didn't do nothing for her."

"What could I do, Mike?"

Mike's expression grew hard.

"You didn't do anything for her either, Mike."

"I wasn't the one she would've listened to."

Hammett grunted. Sure, he'd left her money for treatment, but that hadn't amounted to much—to anything, really. "She wouldn't have listened to me any more than to anybody else. It's not that simple. You know that. The stuff had a hold of her."

Mike grinned.

"Besides, that's my personal life," Hammett said. "I know I've been a bastard to some good people who didn't deserve it. I'm not proud of it. But we're not talking about our personal lives now."

"Oh, your spotless professional life?"

Hammett drank. He'd had enough of Mike.

"You can't have forgotten what we did together to those strikers up in Montana before we ever got to San Francisco? The beatings we handed out? I wouldn't be surprised if some of those poor suckers were . . . well, never the same again. Those kinds of beatings weren't strictly legal, even coming from Pinkertons."

"I'm ashamed of that."

"Are you saying you're ashamed of your association with me?"

"No, I'm ashamed of myself."

Mike said nothing.

"Some of those things from the past make me sick," Hammett said. "I can't go back to those ways."

"OK, so why don't you just tell me how I can get the rock?"

"The 'fake' Falcon your client thinks is real? The 'authentic' counterfeit?"

Mike ran his palm along the top of his bald head as if straightening hairs that were no longer there. "Why are you giving me such a hard time, Sam? This ought to be easy."

"Nothing's easy anymore, Mike. Haven't you noticed?" He didn't wait for an answer. "Sorry, but I can't help you."

Mike glared at Hammett and then slapped his hand down on the bar. "You mean you *won't* help me."

The barkeep and a handful of others looked their way.

Hammett had had enough. "Suit yourself."

Mike leaned casually against the bar. "OK, Sam. That's all right. I respect your decision."

"Glad to hear it."

"It's not as if my livelihood depends entirely on any one client."

"Of course not."

"I got other jobs too."

"Why wouldn't you? You're a hell of a detective, Mike. I never doubted that."

Mike drank. "I'm doing some work for a government agency that I can't name just now. It's steady work. And it's going to be steady for some time. Believe me, it's nice getting a paycheck that you don't have to worry about bouncing when you take to the bank."

"Government work?"

"Off the books, but like I said . . . steady."

Hammett knew where he stood with the government—not good. He didn't want to hear any more. "Goodbye, Mike."

Mike grabbed his forearm. "Stay here, Sam."

Hammett jerked away, but did not move to go.

Mike grinned. "You ever heard of a senator from Wisconsin named Joe McCarthy?"

Of course he'd heard of him. McCarthy was a Red-baiting son of a bitch whose star was ascendant.

"You a Commie, Sam?"

Hammett said nothing.

"That's what some people are saying," Mike continued.

"People say lots of things."

"There sure were a lot of Reds in that class of yours tonight. I noted them. It's my job to do so."

"You haven't learned a damn thing since those strikebreaking days."

"Sure I have, Sam. I've learned that we were *right* to beat the hell out of those agitators. Don't you understand how dangerous the world is? The Russians might have the bomb."

"Don't play the patriot, Mike. You're in it for the money."

"I'm a professional."

"Go to hell."

"Wait, Sam. I want to help you. You're going to need a friend on the inside. I'm your man. We go way back, right? Come on. I don't want to see you ruined. Just tell me where that little black bird is and I'll get you out of the jam that's coming for you."

Hammett noted a whiskey bottle within his reach across the bar. If needed, he could grab it by the neck and backhand his old partner across the face. He hoped he wouldn't need it, but he was willing to take his chances.

"I knew I could talk some sense into you." Mike smiled, misinterpreting Hammett's silence. "We go way back."

"That's true, Mike. All you want from me is the truth?"

"That's all I'm asking, Sam."

"Maybe it'll feel good to get it off my chest."

Mike removed a notepad from his jacket. He licked the sharp point of his pencil. "Go on."

"OK, you know that business in *The Maltese Falcon* about Spade sleeping with Archer's wife?"

Mike looked up from his notepad.

"Look, I made up some stuff when I was writing that book. I changed names and fictionalized the thing, right? That's the job. I'm a professional, too. But the part about Spade sleeping with his partner's wife? That was real, Mike."

Mike's thick Adam's apple moved up and then dropped like a stone in his throat. His eyes narrowed.

Hammett eyed the bottle.

Mike took a deep breath and then put his notepad and pencil back in his jacket. "You've made a big mistake."

"How could I be mistaken about a recollection like that?"

Mike stood. "You Commie son of a bitch."

Hammett turned away. "Goodbye, Mike."

"You'll be hearing from us."

Hammett shrugged as he started out of the bar. What were they going to do, throw him in jail?

TIME MAGAZINE

OCTOBER 22, 1951
JOSEPH McCARTHY

For a moment, Hammett thinks he might have achieved the perfect balance. The right quantities of gin, dry vermouth, orange bitters, and a cocktail onion of perfect proportion in place of an olive. But when he tastes it again he concludes that it is still missing some ingredient, it is still just a well-made martini appropriate for drinking anytime after four o'clock in the afternoon—hell, anytime after eleven in the morning, ten, nine . . . Over the years, he has tried writing sober and he has tried writing drunk and he has tried writing while in every state in between. But earlier this morning as he settled on the porch of Lily's lovely country house he wondered if it might always have been less a question of finding the proper state of inebriation and more a question of finding the proper drink. Might there be an elixir to stimulate a spark in some otherwise sleeping part of his brain? He's heard all the stories about absinthe and marijuana but neither has had an effect on his writing state of mind. So maybe if he adds a radical dash of grenadine to his current concoction. . . . On second thought, no to grenadine—he's not making a goddamn Shirley Temple. (Though maybe making Shirley Temple herself, since she's old enough now to think about in that way—ah, but that sort of thing hasn't worked as a creative catalyst either.) So perhaps, in place of grenadine, he can add an unusual garnish: a coffee bean, a marigold, a cocktail shrimp, a pickled green bean, a spear of asparagus. Naturally, he's already experimented with straight liquor, but that's useful only for recreational, medicinal, and spiritual improvement—not writing. Now, he's drunk off his ass and it's not even lunchtime. Busy morning with all this mixing. He's a regular worker bee. Why can't Lily appreciate that? She should have known the day would turn out this way, just as she should have known better than to leave this week's *Time* magazine sitting on the kitchen table beside the Kellogg's Corn Flakes box—that bastard Joseph McCarthy's picture on the cover (the magazine, not the cereal box). Should have known . . . Straight gin for the rest of the day—or at least until the feds come to get him.

So give us characters as grounded as your readers, but situations that soar to the heights of your imaginings!
—Dashiell Hammett, from an article published in
The Young Writer's Monthly Journal, August 1927

ASHLAND, KENTUCKY & NEW YORK CITY, 1951–52

During his first week as an inmate behind the twenty-foot high, barbed-wire crested walls of the Federal Penitentiary in Ashland, Kentucky, Hammett was reunited in the recreation yard with Emil Madrid, one of the Black Falcon conspirators arrested thirty years before. The afternoon was unseasonably mild, the skies beautiful. Hammett found it impossible to regard the sunshine as anything but an ironic comment, not only on the dreariness of the prison but also on his state of mind, which had been clouded since his arrival, struggling to process the dismal fact of his actually being here. Meantime, the small but flamboyant Emil Madrid emerged grinning from a group of inmates who stood near the softball diamond watching younger cons playing ball.

"What's the matter, Mr. Hammett?" Madrid asked as he approached. "Don't you know me?"

At first, Hammett didn't recognize Madrid, but merely looked him over, saying nothing. Hammett's fame made him a target for cranks. Prison was no different, except worse.

"Don't I look enough like Peter Lorre for you to know who I am?"

In fact, the small Levantine looked very much like Lorre—similarly expressive, saucer-wide eyes, the same delicate skin, sensuous lips, and a fragile, vaguely damaged carriage. And he sounded like him too, his voice breathy, his pronunciation accented. Hammett stepped toward him. "Madrid?"

Madrid nodded.

Hammett had never seen him dressed in anything but the most fastidious and effete of attire.[4] Now, in his faded prison jeans and standard-issue work-shirt, Madrid looked like a wrinkled scarecrow. The little man was close to seventy but looked closer to eighty. The ravages of prison, Hammett thought. He almost felt sorry for him until he realized that Madrid could be thinking the same of Hammett—a once dapper scarecrow dressed now in ill-fitting prison clothing, who looked older than his years.

"I would extend my hand to shake," Madrid said, "except that I recall you have a rather unfortunate habit of slugging me on such occasions."

"Hello, Madrid."

They didn't shake hands but drew nearer one another.

"I never expected to meet you in a place like this," Madrid confided. "A prison exercise yard, with a number stenciled over your heart! But then, being a detective is not so far from being a criminal, is it?"

"It's been a long time since I was a detective."

"Ah yes, you have become a writer. Quite famous, too. I've read your books. Well, being a writer amounts to the same thing as being a detective. In terms of being essentially criminal, I mean. Writers steal people's lives. Is that not so?"

"It's been a long time since I've been a writer."

"Then what have you been doing all these years?"

Hammett had no heart to consider the question—not after the events of the past two years, during which the bastard Joseph McCarthy had gone after him, the IRS had destroyed his finances, the government had placed his name on its "blacklist" (making impossible any new radio or movie adaptations of old work), and countless "civic-minded" groups had insisted on the removal of his novels from the shelves of public libraries. And no new writing. He turned from Madrid toward the softball diamond to watch the ballplayers. Wretched and hard, they played without baseball gloves, stabbing at line drives with bare hands.

"What did you do to end up here?" Madrid asked.

"I'm not 'ending' up here," Hammett snapped. "Six months'll be easy enough."

"Nothing's easy here."

Madrid was right. But Hammett wasn't ready to admit as much—not even to himself. As it was, he managed only two or three hours of sleep each night on the inch-thick pad in his cell, agitated in the darkness by something like despair. By day, he reminded himself it could be worse here. For example, in deference to Hammett's age, the warden had assigned him the job of swabbing out latrines rather than forcing him to labor at a more physically rigorous position in the laundry, foundry, or kitchen. "There's nothing going on here that I can't handle," he said.

"Handle, as in 'broom handle' or 'mop handle'?" Madrid giggled.

"Ah, news spreads fast in here," Hammett observed, put off more by the small man's effeminate laugh than his needling.

"Well, it's not every day that a well-known writer arrives in our cell block to scrub out our piss stains."

Hammett looked back toward the softball game.

"What law did you break?" Madrid pressed.

"Ask Joseph McCarthy."

"The puppet?"

Hammett turned back to him. "What?"

"You know, on the radio. They let us listen to reward good behavior. Sunday nights. Edgar Bergen and Joseph McCarthy."

"That's *Charlie* McCarthy," Hammett said. "Don't you know who Senator Joseph McCarthy is?"

Madrid shook his head no.

"You don't read the newspapers?"

"Why should I? News is nothing to me. Nothing changes here, except, of course, for the occasional celebrity janitor."

"How long have you been inside, Madrid?"

"Since the last time you saw me, Mr. Hammett. Twenty-nine years, seven months, and four days. All thanks to you. But I'm not complaining. I know I was lucky not to have gotten the chair."

Hammett figured it wasn't too much to give the aggravating little man an answer to his question. "I'm here because I was convicted of contempt of court."

"Which means?"

"A judge ordered me to give names of others who, like myself, have committed no offense, except to have a left-leaning political view. On constitutional grounds, I refused."

The little man rubbed at his face with his dirty palm. "Ah, then you're a political prisoner, Mr. Hammett. Oh, we had many political prisoners in my native country. Prisoners of conscience. Yours is a brave stance."

Hammett shook his head no. He thought of his old strikebreaking days. "The feds were wrong to put me in here for standing up to them. But I still deserve whatever I get."

"Very hard-boiled, my famous friend."

"You and I were never friends, Madrid."

"Tell me, Mr. Hammett, how did your colleagues in Hollywood come to the absurd conclusion that I was similar in any way whatsoever to the actor Peter Lorre?"

Hammett thought that of all the actors in the movie, Lorre had been most like his counterpart.

"You cannot have liked the movie yourself," Madrid observed.

"I liked it all right."

"You're probably required contractually to say that."

"No."

"Well, we were all fools back in San Francisco. Traipsing about in pursuit of the Falcon."

"I don't know that I'd describe the killing that went on there as 'traipsing.'"

Madrid ignored the observation. "Yes, fools. All of us."

Hammett didn't disagree about the foolishness.

On the softball diamond, one of the players hit a long fly ball that almost cleared the prison wall. An outfielder ran after it to play the carom, but the ball stuck in the barbwire ten feet above his reach. After a moment of confusion, the teams erupted in argument over whether the hit was a ground rule double or a home run.

"It's not a home run unless it gets out of here," Hammett muttered to himself.

Madrid ignored the disagreement on the diamond, even when the shouting turned to pushing and shoving near home plate. The little man had seen it all before. To him it was routine, even boring (unless somebody pulled a shank). But Hammett watched. The guards moved as a unit onto the field to break up the fight. They bloodied and beat disagreeable softball players, each of whom had to be carried from the diamond before the game could recommence.

"At least you made something of the Falcon mess," Madrid said, tapping at Hammett's shoulder to reclaim his attention. "You made a book out of it. And a great deal of money."

Hammett turned back to him. "That was a long time ago."

"Yes," Madrid continued, "but despite your fame and fortune you were the biggest fool of all, Mr. Hammett. Oh, some of us are dead and others of us have wasted away in prison but you had the actual Falcon for all those years and then you gave it away."

Not this, not now. "You too, Madrid?"

The little man poked Hammett's chest with his index finger. "I know all about you."

Hammett pushed his hand away. "You know nothing about me."

"Ah, but I do." He grinned. "See, Moira came here just days after she got out of the loony bin. That would have been back in '31 or '32."

"'33," Hammett said.

"Whichever." With a delicate hand, Madrid waved away the distinction between years. "She stopped here on her way to New York City, where she planned to talk you out of the bird by telling you the truth, of all things! Believe me, her determination was palpable."

Hammett hadn't forgotten Moira's determination at the Hotel Pierre. "Are you asking me if that's what happened?"

Madrid shook his head no. "I already know that's what happened."

"How?"

Madrid took a deep breath. "Well, it's true I didn't hear anything about it for a very long time." He rubbed his hands together. "Actually, it wasn't until a few years ago, when your old cohort Mike Arnette visited me to ask questions about Moira. He said you claimed to have given her the statuette. He suspected you were lying to him. But I knew you weren't. I knew Moira had carried through with her plan. Oh, I can't say I was happy she actually wound up with the thing, the conniving bitch. But I won't deny I was heartily gratified to learn you'd lost it, Mr. Hammett."

Hammett stepped toward the little man. "Do you know where she is?"

Madrid stepped back. "She only came here that one time."

"And since then?"

"What do you think, Mr. Hammett, she sends me Christmas cards?"

Hammett wasn't going to tell Madrid about the fruitless inquiries he'd made to track her down. "But when she came here, you believed her hokum?"

"Oh, I always believed it, Mr. Hammett. Because it's not hokum, it's true. I heard it from the Russian himself. In Saint Petersburg, around 1905, just before he took the thing and went on the lam. Of course, I didn't give up. No, it took seventeen years, but the Big Man and I finally tracked him down and separated him from the statuette." He stopped. His expression changed in the course of three heartbeats, from reverie to discomfort to anger. He clenched his small fists. "Seventeen *years* to search that Russian bastard out! And even after we found him . . . well, you don't know half of what we had to do to get the thing away from him. And then, after we arranged for its transport to San Francisco, via Hong Kong for God's sake, *you* had to stumble onto the scene at the last moment to spoil everything."

Hammett wasn't interested in the details of the old caper. "So you say you were never after a 'jeweled' bird?"

Madrid dismissed the assertion with another wave of his hand. "Moira and I just pretended. I don't know how she learned about the bird. But we kept our knowledge of the thing's mystical nature a secret, not only from fools like you but even from the Big Man, who believed to the end that there was actually a jeweled statuette."

Hammett wondered if Madrid knew the Big Man was still alive. "It's a shame about what happened to Gaspereaux."

Madrid turned and spat on the ground. "He got what he deserved."

"I guess we all do," Hammett said.

Madrid shook his head no. "You got years of good fortune that you were never entitled to, Mr. Hammett."

He'd heard enough. "Leave me alone, Madrid."

"OK, for the time being."

Hammett watched the little man make his way back toward the softball game.

A few weeks later in the windowless, ammonia-scented cement room that served as the prison library (thirty feet by thirty feet with one long steel table in the middle, six wooden stools aligned on each side), Hammett was interrupted in his reading by a gentle tap on his shoulder. He jumped, his nerves frayed by too many long nights and boring, sinister days, and turned around. It was Madrid.

"I see you're reading Wolfram von Eschenbach's *Parzival*," the small man observed.

Hammett closed the book, face down, on the steel table. "Just browsing."

"Thirteenth-century source material for the Grail myths," Madrid said, picking up a second book from Hammett's pile. "Ah, and *The Mabinogion*," he read aloud. "What a coincidence! I know that one, too. Ancient Welsh stories, some of which speak of a stone with limitless powers . . ."

"Research for a new novel," Hammett explained.

Madrid laughed. "Don't you mean research for a book you already wrote?"

"What would you know, Madrid?"

"Plenty."

"Do you mind if I return to my reading?"

Madrid ignored the question. He glanced at the sagging shelves on one wall, where the library's entire collection—second-hand books that numbered no more than a few hundred—were stacked in haphazard order. "Isn't it commendable," Madrid asked, "that this good federal institution would provide such unusual books as these two for us inmates to read?"

"Obviously, I ordered the books from a shop," Hammett said.

Madrid nodded, knowingly.

"Look, Madrid, this mumbo jumbo is just a way to pass the time."

Madrid sat beside him. "May I make a suggestion?"

Hammett said nothing.

"You must go further back in history, Mr. Hammett, if you're going to discover the true nature of the Black Falcon."

"Look, I don't give a damn about the thing."

"Whatever Moira told you, she only knew half of it."

"She was certifiable, literally."

Madrid cringed. "It is both cruel and inaccurate of you to say such a thing. She was a bitch, yes. But not insane. That was just the plea she copped."

"What do you want, Madrid?"

"I want to help you understand the Falcon."

"Why?"

"Revenge, I suppose."

"I see." Hammett hardly blamed him. He looked around the room, which was unoccupied but for an elderly inmate who dozed at the end of the reading table and a disinterested guard who sat near the door, leafing through a copy of *Life* magazine. "OK, Madrid. Tell me about the Black Falcon."

"May I sit with you?"

Hammett shook his head no.

"But you'll listen, Mr. Hammett?"

He'd be damned if he allowed himself to seem interested. "Two minutes."

"Oh, how I wish I had my journal, Mr. Hammett. You see, years ago I wrote everything down. In code, of course. I fully explicated the black bird's background. At least, to the extent that I was able. Oh, how I wish I had that damn book! I would simply give it to you to read. But it was lost decades ago."

"You have a minute and forty seconds left," Hammett said, glancing at his watch.

"Oh yes, yes." Madrid gathered himself, his hands fluttering about. "But first, Mr. Hammett, may I ask you something?"

"Ask."

"When Moira visited you in New York, did she describe the Black Falcon's exalted status among the Crusaders?"

"She said something about that."

Madrid lightly clapped his hands, smirking. "Yes, she told me she was going to use the *truth*, of all things, to make both her acquisition and your humiliation all the sweeter."

Hammett tapped his watch. "You're wasting your time."

Madrid rubbed his hands together. "And did she tell you that the Knights Templar brought the statuette back to England after acquiring it in the Holy Land, where they discovered it in their excavation of the ancient Temple of Solomon?"

"Yes, some such yarn."

"And she explained how the earliest Grail myths speak of a stone, rather than a cup?"

"Yes."

"Well, she was wrong. The Black Falcon is not the Holy Grail."

Hammett laughed. "Thank you, but I surmised that myself, Emil."

"Still, it is an object of enormous mystical power."

"You have a minute-twenty."

Madrid took a deep breath and set his posture like a child at the head of the class. "The sculpture was indeed recovered by the Crusaders but not from the ruins of the temple. No, the Knights Templar took it from a sect of Arabs who had possessed it for countless generations. The sect believed the black stone had powers one can describe only as . . ." He stopped, searching for the word.

"May I suggest, as a former professional writer, that the word you're looking for is 'unbelievable'?" Hammett said.

Madrid looked away, frustrated.

Hammett couldn't keep from needling Madrid. "You have one minute, Emil."

"To understand the true significance of the Black Falcon, you must understand its origins, which predate the Crusades by many centuries. The bird is far older than either Christianity or Islam. Its history reaches to the earliest religion of the Arabs, which involved the worship of gods associated with heavenly bodies."

"Bodies like Rita Hayworth's?" Hammett asked.

"Like the moon and sun," Madrid answered huffily.

"Next you'll tell me the Aztecs figure in all this."

"That's not fair, Mr. Hammett! Your snide remarks are very distracting. They should not count against my arbitrary time limit."

"OK, Madrid. I'll give you another minute."

"OK then. Now, where was I?"

"Sky gods."

"Oh, yes. Now, tell me, Mr. Hammett, have you ever heard of *baetyls*?"

In fact, Hammett had read a little about ancient Levantine mythology. But he shook his head no as if he had not.

"Baetyls are stones that contain magical powers," Madrid said. "In the Hebrew language, *betyl* means meteorite. The equivalent word in Greek is *baitylia*, which translates as 'the residence of God.'"

"You should seek work with the Oxford English Dictionary," Hammett said.

Madrid ignored him. "The point is, Mr. Hammett, these stones come from the sky. Today, we call them meteorites and we believe we understand them. But the ancient Arabs believed these stones possessed cosmic forces and that some of them contained the spirits of gods. Naturally, such stones were venerated."

"Naturally," Hammett said.

"I will not be put off by your skeptical attitude, Mr. Hammett! Or should I say, by your ignorance."

Hammett put his hands to his heart. "You cut me to the quick, Madrid."

"I demand another full minute!"

The guard looked up from his *Life* magazine, his eyes narrowed in a threatening squint. The elderly inmate didn't awaken.

Hammett lowered his voice. "Fine, Madrid, another minute."

Once more, Madrid took a deep breath before starting. "The ancient Arabs believed that mere proximity to a baetyl induced good fortune. I doubt, Mr. Hammett, that you've ever heard of Manat, the ancient Arabian goddess of fate and destiny."

This was a new one to him. "Go on, Madrid."

"Manat was the personification of the evening star, one of the daughters of the pre-Islamic Allah. The word *mana* is still used by Arabs to mean 'luck.' Manat's cult was situated on the road between Mecca and Medina where she was worshiped in the form of a black stone."

"And the stone was a symbol of the goddess?"

"You know better than that, Mr. Hammett. You know it was no symbol. The spirit of the goddess herself was contained in the stone."

Hammett said nothing.

"The goddess of fate and destiny," Madrid continued. "In the black stone."

"Which you're going to suggest was later carved into the shape of a falcon."

"Exactly, Mr. Hammett. Unless, that is, the black stone arrived here on Earth already possessed of its aviary form, which is quite possible, considering its cosmic source."

"Cosmic source," Hammett scoffed. Nonetheless, this was yet another absurdity to set among all the others, which singly were laughable, though when taken together. . . . Hammett wasn't pleased with the thought. Maybe being in this windowless, tomb-like chamber (library my ass, he thought) weakened his native sensibility. Maybe being one of the walking dead in this vast, federally-run mausoleum had muddled him. In any case, he picked up one of the books set on the table before him and waved it at Madrid, forsaking any further hope of seeming disengaged from the little Levantine's mythological ravings. "And what about this, Madrid?"

"What is that book, Mr. Hammett?"

"It's about an ancient Chaldean sun god."

"Well, there are other . . . ," Madrid started.

Hammett didn't let him finish, but instead opened the book to a marked page and read aloud: "Since the time of the Hittites, numerous mountain gods have been depicted as falcons." He flipped ahead to another marked page. "In the ancient city of Emesa, the followers of the god Elegabal worshipped a black stone, believed by the Roman historian Herodian to be a meteorite. This worship involved rites associated with an even more ancient Babylonian god, Gibil, whose name not only means 'god of the black stone' but may also refer to a Semitic root that means 'to create.'"

Hammett stopped when he noticed Madrid grinning. He dropped the book carelessly onto the pile of others on the table.

"So you *are* interested," Madrid observed.

Hammett shook his head no. "I only wanted to demonstrate that your little yarn about Manat is nothing special, but is as derivative as an episode of *The Lone Ranger*."

Madrid sat down, unbidden but emboldened. "Yes, but so too is your Babylonian version, Mr. Hammett. And that is neither here nor there, because the real question is not which among all the stories is factual, but to what unknown fact do all of the stories refer?"

Hammett couldn't help but be impressed by Madrid's response.

"Yes, Mr. Hammett, each culture that encountered this stone over the ages explained it in its own way. But that doesn't mean the powers of the stone are not real."

Hammett pushed his chair away from the table and stood. "You actually believe this, Madrid? I thought you were a man of the world."

Madrid looked up at him. "I am. But there is more than one world. Oh, we may think of ourselves as moderns, but the cosmos is unmoved by our pretensions. To the gods, time is nothing. Believe me, however one chooses to define it, the black bird controls fate and destiny."

Hammett said nothing, but set his weight against the table.

Madrid continued: "To possess the Falcon is, quite simply, the most direct means of insuring a successful destiny, whatever 'success' may mean to whomever possesses it. That is why the bird has been sought so avidly by those who've understood its nature."

"Ours is an age of science, Madrid. Not superstition."

"Science? Fair enough. But much of what is regarded as science today was thought to be mere superstition in the past. For example, is it not true that sixty years ago you would have scoffed at the possibility that certain stones can emanate invisible radiation, sometimes powerful enough to heal or to kill? Well?"

"Without proof, yes."

"Yet Madame Curie discovered such emanations in pitch blend and was awarded the Nobel Prize for it. What do you say to that?"

"She proved her discovery through the experimental method."

"Yes, just as the power of the Black Falcon has now been proved!"

"How?"

"I was a doubter once myself," Madrid said. "But you, Mr. Hammett, have proven the stories about the stone's powers to be true."

"Me?"

"A simple review of your personal history indicates that as long as the statuette sat on your writing desk, you prospered. Stories and then books rattled out of your typewriter. But after you gave the bird away . . . Well, I've followed your career. Is it mere coincidence that in the time you possessed the Falcon you produced great quantities of writing? And is it mere coincidence that since you gave away the Falcon you've produced nothing?"

"Your time is up, Madrid," Hammett said, standing.

"Yes, but your time has been up since the day you gave the Falcon away."

Hammett attempted to smile, but he could no longer pretend that the joke was on Madrid.

The little man grinned and wiped sweat from his brow with a flowered handkerchief. "You can get back to your reading, Mr. Hammett. Of course, I can't imagine what interest it could hold for you, considering you're such a 'man of the world,' such a skeptic, such a . . . let's see, what was that word you used in your famous book? A *sap*. Yes, that's it."

"Leave me alone."

Madrid grinned and obliged.

Hammett didn't talk to him again during his time in Ashland.

Ancient Babylonian, Arab, or Egyptian gods inhabiting and empowering a black stone, the nature of which had been transposed in the Christian era to a sacred object of life-giving Grail powers, all adding up to a gumshoe from Baltimore temporarily finding fulfillment writing acclaimed mystery novels? What pulp nonsense! Hammett recognized Madrid's taunting as a weapon that the little Levantine wielded against him. And as such, Hammett had to admit it was a damn sight better than the ordinary, bitter curses spoken by other criminals he'd put behind bars.

Still, he couldn't help wondering if there was more to it.

What was a modern to make of it?

Hammett's old drinking buddy William Faulkner wore a particular sweater whenever he sat down at his typewriter to work; presumably, the sweater helped him to focus his attention. There wasn't anything magical about the sweater, but it held ritualistic value, whether or not Faulkner admitted to such an anthropological explanation. (He had once laughed at Hammett's suggestion that Yoknapatawpha County might not exist if the old sweater had been knitted with a less sturdy weave.) Additionally, Hammett could name countless baseball players who stuck wads of gum on the inside bill of their hats or avoided stepping on chalked lines to ensure good luck in their games. Of course, such practices were mere exercises in psychology—not mysticism. But what might happen if Faulkner was denied his sweater? Or if Enos Slaughter was forbidden from spitting into his palms before taking his licks at home plate?

"That's absurd," Lillian said a few months later when Hammett expressed his creeping suspicions over lunch at Sardi's in New York City, where they'd gone to celebrate his release from Ashland.

It was a long way from federal prison.

But some things hadn't changed.

"Faulkner's sweater?" Lily mused, doubtfully.

They occupied a corner booth, away from other diners but still hemmed tight by framed caricatures of Broadway notables that populated the walls. Naturally, Lillian's caricature was among them, her exaggerated features enshrined near the foyer between Mary Martin and Oscar Hammerstein. There had once been a caricature of Hammett too, hung near the bar, but he'd made known to the proprietor his low opinion of such "clubby," adolescent honors and the drawing was eventually removed.[5]

"Bubble gum on the bill of a ballplayer's cap?" Lily pressed. She picked up the saltshaker, tapping it nervously on the table. The line of her jaw was set straight and serious. "You've gone around the bend, Dash."

"Bring me another drink," Hammett instructed the cocktail waitress.

"This writer's block is driving you mad," Lily observed.

"Put the goddamn saltshaker down," he said. "And I'm not 'blocked.'"

"Well, whatever you want to call it."

"Call it anything but 'blocked.'"

She picked up her smoldering cigarette and took a long drag. "OK, let's call it 'nothing.'"

"It's been twenty years, Lily. It's not nothing."

She nodded and blew smoke. "OK, so you're blocked."

Hammett knew it was a mistake to engage this conversation with Lily. It put her in a difficult position; she was still writing successful plays (which paid for their meals at restaurants like this). He didn't expect her to provide him with answers or consolation; nonetheless, he felt the need to press these things onto someone—and if not onto her, then who? He looked at her face. It had always been grand—if never pretty. Over the years it had seemed to harden to stone, deeply etched as if by the elements. His affairs with other women had been part of that hardening, no doubt. But here they were, still lunching together after all these years. That was something, at least. He watched her open her menu, though he knew she had long ago consigned all the choices to memory.

"Perhaps crab cakes," she said.

Yes, changing the subject was judicious. But he didn't care. A quote entered his mind. He spoke it aloud. "'A man cannot say, 'I will compose poetry.' Poetry is the product of some invisible influence, like an inconstant wind."

Lillian looked up, confused.

"It's Shelley," he said.

She put the menu back on the white tablecloth and took another long drag on her cigarette. "You've got to give it to those Romantics—they really knew how to suffer."

Hammett shrugged.

"Why do you know that quote, Dash?"

"Because I read, Lily."

"Yes, I read too." She crushed the end of her cigarette in the ashtray. She opened her purse and removed another cigarette. A waiter moved to the table to light the cigarette for her. "I know what you're experiencing is painful," she said.

"I'm not looking for sympathy."

"I understand. But Dash . . . I'm not going to apologize to you for the fact that I'm still writing."

"I'm not asking you to do that."

"Why strain for explanations when critics are so willing to provide them for you?"

"The critics are full of shit."

She ignored him. "Let's see, Dash," she said. "Some critics attribute your absence from the world of letters to your disillusionment with the detective genre. And others attribute it to your involvement in leftist politics and your current persecution by our 'ever-watchful' federal government. And others attribute it to your drinking and womanizing. And still others to your long relationship with me, who, after all, entered your life an unknown and emerged shortly thereafter a well-tutored practitioner of American drama who, they suggest, drained the great Hammett of his powers. Explanations enough?"

"They're none of them right," he said. "Or maybe all of them are right. Still, there's something else."

"What?"

"I've done a little research."

"That black stone again?"

He looked away. How could he make her understand what he didn't understand himself? Actually, what was there to understand, at least in terms of rationality? "I'm not saying I believe it," he said.

"You're not?"

"Hell, no."

She leaned back in the booth. "For a minute you had me worried."

"What do you think I've become, Lily?" He took a long drink from his water glass. "I did time in a penitentiary, not a mental institute, for God's sake. I'm just suggesting this talisman business as a setup for a new story."

"That could work."

He nodded. "A desperate character taking desperate measures."

"Good. Write it, Dash."

If only it were that simple, he thought.

THE AMERICAN
MAGAZINE

DECEMBER 1908
"A NEW STORY OF
SHERLOCK HOLMES"

Sam opens his eyes to find his mother standing at the foot of his bed. It is morning. Has he overslept again? It'd be no wonder, seeing as he stayed up late last night, reading by the light of an electric torch for many hours after he heard his mother retire from the parlor to the bedroom she shares with his wheezing, sick father. Since the old man's illness, she's stopped coming into Sam's room to say goodnight. That's all right. He's fourteen years old, after all. And even if she did come in to find him reading under the covers, she'd not object. She loves books too, especially mysteries. When he was younger, she used to brag to her friends about how many books he read. Of course, his schoolwork has always been another matter. He's not much interested by sums and memorization, so his grades are not so good. Now he sits up in his bed, rubbing his eyes to see her clearer. She looks down at him with a grim expression and tells him his father is too sick to work anymore. Sam wonders if that means his father is too sick to get drunk anymore, too sick to go off with strange women, too sick to knock his only son around the house? That would make his father's being sick not such a bad thing. His mother sits on the end of the bed. She says it is time Sam gets a job to support the family, pointing out that his truancy and shoddy schoolwork indicate his disinterest in education anyway. When he tries to explain himself, she shushes him and stands. When he's gainfully employed at the railroad yard, there'll be no more tardiness, she says. Therefore, there'll be no more late night reading. She goes to his small desk and gathers into her arms his current crop of books and magazines, including the latest issue of *The American Magazine*, which contains the new Sherlock Holmes story. He climbs out of bed. What are you doing, Mother? I'm disposing of these things, she answers. You can't be late to your new job the way you've been late so often for school. You're a man now, and so you mustn't be distracted anymore by useless fantasies. When he objects, she turns to him, her eyes half-crazed. These books are of no use to you, she says. Look around at us. Look around at yourself, for God's sake! Books are for other people, smarter people. When he reminds her that she's often said she's proud of all the books he brings home from the library, she shakes her head no. She says she was only pretending—that in truth watching him read all those books always made her worry that he was a good-for-nothing weakling. He feels his heart pounding, his face hot. Is this a nightmare? Then he notices she is crying. When he asks her why, she tells him it is because she is sad to consider all the time he's wasted these past years reading books when he is truly only suited to work in the railroad yards or maybe on the docks with the crabbers. She tells him it is time to face the facts about life and himself.

NEW YEAR'S EVE, 1959

Now Hammett was a dying man for whom climbing a flight of stairs posed serious problems. But he was also a former detective whose specialty had been recovering missing persons and stolen objects, which explained his presence here, inside the Paxton residence of King's Point, New York. A missing person, a stolen object. True, it had been a lucky break that led him here rather than actual detective work. But what did that matter? He was here—New Year's Eve, likely his last. Out with the old, in with the new. And though this was not St. Petersburg, Constantinople, Hong Kong, San Francisco, nor any other previously known locale of the statuette, it was the right place.

Moira stood on the landing, halfway up the staircase, her eyes wide at the sight of the gun.

"Look, what do you want?" she asked.

She had to be over sixty now, but she didn't look it. Somehow, she hadn't lost her allure—red hair, blue eyes, long legs. He noted the tilt of her hip where she placed one hand, and the proud set of her chin, a socialite posture. It worked for her, he thought, particularly as she couldn't very well play the ingénue anymore. Despite the complication, he was not altogether sorry she'd shown up. He liked seeing her—he always had, goddamn it.

"It's me, Hammett."

"Who?"

"Dashiell Hammett."

"The *writer*?"

He nodded, though he'd been no writer for decades.

"Jesus, you *are* him. I've seen your picture in the paper."

"Look, I know who you are, Mrs. Paxton." He pronounced the name with ironic emphasis. "You don't have to pretend."

"Why are you here?"

"Come downstairs and we'll discuss it."

She didn't move. "What do you want?"

"Only to take back what's mine."

"I don't understand."

"Let's not play games."

"You're the one with the gun," she snapped. "What kind of game is that?"

He didn't lower the gun. "I didn't intend for it to be this way. You were supposed to be out at a party."

"I have a head cold."

"Tea will help that. With a little bourbon."

She gathered her satin robe tighter around her body. "You say you know who I am?"

"You know perfectly well that I do."

She shook her head no.

"Please, Moira. No games."

"Who's Moira?"

"Cut the crap. I know who you are and you know what I've come for."

She looked hard at him, her gaze disconcertingly fearless. "You don't understand, Mr. Hammett. I *don't* know what you want. And while I recognize your name and face because you're a public figure, I don't know you. Maybe I did once, but I don't anymore. See, my memory is . . ." She stopped, looking around the entryway as if seeking for a word hidden in some corner. "My memory is incomplete."

He stepped toward the staircase. "What does that mean?"

"I've waited a long time for someone to come through that door who knew me from before."

"Before what?"

"Before I became who I am now," she answered, balling her hands into fists.

"What are you talking about?"

"Before 1933."

"You mean before you got the bird?"

"Bird?"

He didn't have time for this. "You know damn well what I mean."

She took a step downstairs, then another. "I've been waiting a long time to meet someone who knew me before I got hurt."

"Hurt?"

She straightened her silk cover-up. "Almost killed."

"Explain yourself," he said.

She took a deep breath and laced her fingertips together over her heart. "A car took a corner too fast," she said, matter-of-factly. She looked down at him. "At least, that's what I was told. Doctors said I was lucky not to have been killed. But my memories of everything that came before the accident, well . . ." She made a gesture with her hand as of tossing sand onto the wind.

He laughed. Amnesia was strictly for the pulps. "You haven't lost your nerve, Moira."

"No one ever tracked me down," she said, unfazed by his skepticism. "I've never known if anyone was even looking for me. But I always hoped, and now you're here, even if you're crude and ill-mannered."

"Look, why don't you just tell me where I'll find the black bird?"

"Is this some sort of dream?" she asked.

"I don't think so."

She glanced past him, across the entry, and toward a dimly lit sitting room.

"Is it in there?" He leveled the gun at her. He didn't like holding a gun on a woman. But he reminded himself of the unfinished obituary in his pocket and the growing tumor in his lung. Besides, she was well enough acquainted with rough treatment and he suspected she would respond to nothing less. He motioned for her to come downstairs.

"If you know me, why the gun, Mr. Hammett?"

"It's because I know you."

"If I try to run back up the stairs will you shoot me?"

"Don't make me decide."

When she reached the bottom of the staircase she stopped three feet from where he stood. "You say that bird statuette used to belong to you?"

He ignored her question. "You've done all right for yourself, Mrs. Paxton. This house, the grounds, the paintings, the sculpture . . . I congratulate you."

"Well, I don't sleep at night."

"Guilty conscience?"

She shook her head no. "One has to remember things in order to regret them."

"Oh yeah, the amnesia . . . " He tried to figure the angle. It made no sense. But he hadn't come here for stories, either true or false. He'd come for the bird. Nothing else really mattered now. "Where is it, Mrs. Paxton?"

"I don't understand your being here, Mr. Hammett."

"I think you do. But if you don't, don't try."

She indicated a vertical distance of about nine inches between her hands. "Black stone about so big?"

"Yeah."

She led him into the sitting room and flipped on a light. "There," she said, pointing.

At the far end of the room, on the middle shelf of an elaborate china cabinet—between a Lalique horse and a Baccarat cat—sat the Black Falcon, primitive and powerful, but neither more nor less "displayed" than any of the glass figurines or fine Gallé and Daum vases also in the case. (Of course, for eleven years the statuette had been placed just as casually on Hammett's desk, among his pencils and note-pads.) He had forgotten the roughness of its shape, having confused it in his recollection with the more detailed sculpture Huston used in his movie. But he recognized it now.

She opened the glass doors and removed the statuette, dusting it briefly with her fingertips. "It's of no particular artistic interest." She turned toward Hammett, who held the gun now at his side.

"Good, then you won't miss it," he said.

"It's all I have left of my past."

"All the more reason for you to be rid of it."

She moved to him, but she didn't hand over the bird. "What makes this thing so valuable that a man like you would come after it like this?"

"Still with the amnesia?" he asked. He didn't wait for an answer, but took the statuette from her.

It felt solid, ancient.

"You said you knew me," she pressed.

He examined the bird, discerning a small chip near the right eye, as Gaspereaux had believed. But there were also chips near the left eye and elsewhere, as there were bound to be. The thing was very old. Gaspereaux's ravings meant little or nothing. What mattered was that Hammett recognized the statuette.

"A few answers aren't so much to ask of you," she snapped, her hands waving about her.

He turned to her. "Look, stay calm."

"Calm? You've assaulted my home, threatened my life, and stolen an object to which I have some sentimental attachment. You can spare me a few minutes of talk!"

He shook his head no. "I didn't come here to talk."

"I'm calling the police," she said, turning away. "I've had enough. You'll have to shoot me or go to jail or give me some answers. This is *my* home, whoever you may once have been to me." She started across the room for a telephone on the desk beside the bookshelf.

"Wait," he said. The lucid Moira would never call the police, not even after all these years. But this wasn't the first time he'd wondered if she'd lost her mind. In any case, he knew the police wouldn't agree with him that *setting things right* justified his breaking-and-entering or his brandishing of a handgun. "You were supposed to be out tonight," he said.

"I don't need you to tell me what I already know."

Now that he had the bird, why not talk to her to calm her down, whatever her angle? "Christ, you were watching the movie when I got here."

"*The Maltese Falcon?*"

He nodded.

"You've lost me, Mr. Hammett."

"I've lost lots of things, Moira. Including this," he said, indicating the stone Falcon.

"That paperweight?"

"Paperweight . . . yeah, sure."

She looked at him, then pointed to the sculpted Falcon, which he gripped so tightly that the tendons in his hands stood out like wires. "Are you trying to strangle that bird?"

He hadn't realized he was holding it so tight.

"Why's it so important that you'd make a fool of yourself like this just to get it?" she asked.

"I thought you wanted to hear about yourself."

"That's right," she said as she settled onto a leather sofa. "So tell me, how do we know each other?"

He put the gun into his coat pocket.

"That weapon makes me sad to consider what kind of relationship we must once have had," she said.

He tried to figure her angle.

"I've hired private detectives," she continued, pressing her palms together as she spoke. "I tried everything to learn about my past. But

I learned nothing. Then again, none of the detectives was Dashiell Hammett."

"It's been a long time since I was a detective."

"Look, I'll happily part with that statuette if you'll just tell me who I was. You say my name was Moira? Moira what?"

"You said you were hit by a car."

"Yes, I still have scars." She leaned forward and flipped her hair to expose a dark ridge of scar tissue at the base of her skull. The scar didn't necessarily make her story true. She might have slipped on an icy sidewalk or been blackjacked in a mugging or any number of possible mishaps. He had an impulse to run his index finger along the scar. He resisted. She sat back and straightened her hair. "I woke up in Lennox Hill Hospital with no memory of how I got there. Or of anything that came before."

"Unusual."

She ran her hands through her thick, disheveled strands of auburn hair. "I know it sounds like something out of a second feature, but it's true. Of course, even at the hospital the doctors kept telling me how rare total amnesia is, as if they could talk me out of the condition by citing statistics. They also assured me I would regain parts of my past. But they were wrong. Nothing's ever come back. Even today, doctors don't seem to quite believe what's happened to me. Good lord, my skull was cracked like an egg! But after twenty-five years they still suggest my memory loss is a 'hysterical, psychosomatic response.' But to what? Why would anybody *want* something like amnesia? Who wants to lose herself, of all things?"

He nodded as if he agreed. But he recalled that the Moira he'd last seen at the Hotel Pierre possessed reasons to want to lose her past, her former self—eleven years in a psych ward, to say nothing of the ruthless indignities that inevitably characterize a life working the grift. He glanced at the statuette in his hand, which she'd possessed all these years. Had this thing made of her a blank slate to facilitate her fresh start? Was that what she had truly wanted (however avaricious and self-satisfied she'd seemed at the time)? He remained wary. Considering the Falcon as a mystical catalyst at work in her life strained credulity. He knew it wasn't viable even as B-movie material. But would he be here now if he hadn't already come to believe that the statuette figured as more than a mere *objet d'art* in the lives of its owners? "You say you remembered nothing when you came out of the coma?"

"That's right. I was unconscious for two and a half weeks. Swelling on the brain, they said. In all, I laid in that hospital for seven weeks, thinking that any minute something would come back to me. I tried concentration exercises and relaxation techniques. But nothing worked. Nothing ever has. Joe hired the first of the private detectives. That was towards the end of my hospitalization, after he and I . . ."

"Dr. Joseph Paxton?" Hammett interrupted.

"My husband. I met him in the hospital. He was my doctor."

A few days before, in the New York City Hall of Records, Hammett had learned that Dr. and Mrs. Joseph Paxton had wed in 1934. Dr. Paxton, a neurosurgeon, would eventually become dean of the Medical School at NYU and later president of the University; further research in the files of the *New York Times* and the *New York World* indicated that Dr. Paxton had died recently of heart failure, leaving behind a wife who, according to the society pages, was an avid fundraiser for charitable causes and also a serious collector of modern art, including the two Matisse drawings Hammett had noticed in the entryway and the paintings by Picasso and Braque that hung on opposite walls in this room. "What did your detectives find out?" he asked.

"Nothing."

If she was lying about this, she was even better at it than she used to be—better than Cletus Gaspereaux, better than Emil Madrid, better than anyone he'd ever met (and he'd met some good ones.) But why would she lie? Hadn't she already handed over the Falcon? "How did this statuette come into your possession, Moira?"

"Moira . . . It's strange to be called by that name."

"Does it seem familiar to you?"

"The name? No."

"How about the bird?"

"Of course it's familiar. It's occupied that same spot since Joe and I moved into this house almost twenty years ago. I was carrying it when I was hit by the car. Or so I'm told."

He waited, unconvinced.

"A good Samaritan picked it up off the pavement and put it in the ambulance when they took me away. Unfortunately, the same cannot be said of my handbag, which contained my identification and was stolen at the scene."

"So the statuette is the only object you have from your past?"

She nodded. "It's not exactly to my taste. Aesthetically speaking, it's rather crude. But I've always thought of it as childlike and so somewhat in keeping with . . . well, perhaps with my own childhood, whatever that was. How does it figure in all this? And by what rights have you come here to take it?"

He stood, agitated. "Where did this automobile accident take place?"

"Manhattan."

"Where?"

"Fifth Avenue at Sixty-first."

He knew what she was going to say next before she said it.

"Just outside the Hotel Pierre." She waited for a response. After a silence, she asked, "Do you know it?"

"Yes."

She straightened. "Were we at the Pierre together?"

"Yes."

"Did you see the accident?"

"No."

"Were we lovers?"

"Not anymore."

She stood, wringing her hands. "So what happened at the Pierre?"

Hammett remembered the late afternoon sunlight casting his writing desk in a warm glow that could not have been more dramatic if it had been lit by gaffers at Warner Bros. Of course, his memory may have been colored by all that followed. The black bird sat on the upper right corner of the desk, overlooking with its inscrutable gaze a legal-size pad of paper that was centered to rows of pencils on either side of the blotter. On the pad were scribbled notes about Nick and Nora Charles, final revisions for their soon-to-be famous adventure. Though the statuette was ugly, he liked having it around. In fact, he'd almost gone after Moira to retrieve the statuette after she left his suite. But how could he explain his attachment to the bird without seeming to confirm her vitriolic verbal assault? So he let it go. Now, he imagined she'd raced out of the elevator, through the lobby and out into the street, distracted by her triumph, where she was hit by a car. Hammett didn't remember hearing ambulance or police sirens that afternoon, but his room was on an upper floor and he might have turned on the radio to distract himself from what he recalled feeling at the time was an appallingly childish sense of loss.

It was possible. "You remember none of it?" he asked.

She shook her head no. "In the hospital they suggested I keep a journal. They thought doing so might stimulate my memory. I've been faithful to daily entries ever since. Well, almost daily. Unfortunately, it's never stirred any memories. Still, it's not without value. If you'd like to see it, I'll show you. I'll get it and show you." She stood.

"Sit down."

"But . . ."

"Sit," he snapped.

She did as she was told.

He looked at her.

If he took the statuette away and the hoodoo that had brought him here was real, what would become of this apparently charitable woman, who in essence might be no more Moira O'Shea than she was Eleanor Roosevelt?

"Are you all right?" she asked. "You look strange."

"I'm fine."

"Well then?"

"Why worry about a past that isn't even your own anymore?" he asked.

"What do you mean 'not my own'?"

"What's it matter who you were before?" he pressed.

"Why do you answer every question I ask with another question?"

"It's an occupational hazard, as a detective and a writer." Actually, he didn't know how to answer her questions—he had no handle on the story.

"Nobody wants to come from nowhere," she said.

On the wall behind her was an arrangement of family photographs. At the center was a wedding picture—Moira with her doctor husband, who looked to have been a pleasant enough man. Other pictures featured the couple in a café in Paris, on a gondola in Venice, in a nightclub in Hollywood, on the Spanish Steps in Rome. "You don't come from nowhere."

She glanced at the pictures, then took a deep breath. "If my life were a play, you could say it's had a reasonably happy act 2. Still, who wants to arrive at the theater at intermission? I mean, without an act 1 . . ." She shrugged, helplessly. "But you can tell me all about that, because you were there."

This evening on the drive up from Manhattan, he had been pleased by the prospect of turning upside down whatever selfish life she'd acquired for herself. But he'd not anticipated the possibility that Moira O'Shea and Mrs. Brigid Paxton might, in essence, be truly different people. He'd hurt many women in his life—Josephine, his former wife; Lily, his companion for all these decades; Evie LeFabre, his friend;

and countless others who'd agreed to play by his rules, which made for games that could end only in their defeat. His daughters belonged on that list, too. And maybe even Moira O'Shea. "I've never treated a woman right in my life."

"You've lied to them?"

He set the Falcon statuette down on her coffee table. "Usually, I played it straight. You know, 'take it or leave it.' Generally, they take it."

"Are you playing it straight with me, Mr. Hammett?"

He didn't know how he was playing it.

"Why did you come *tonight*?" she asked. "Why not next year or twenty years ago?"

"Because I only just learned you were here," he said.

Two weeks before, when he was wheeled into the business office of the Lennox Hill Hospital to sign medical consent forms for some damnable test, he'd glanced up at a framed photograph of the hospital's Board of Directors. There, in professional quality black-and-white, he discovered the long lost Moira O'Shea standing among a dozen gray-haired men in business suits. "What's that woman calling herself these days?" he asked, climbing out of the wheelchair. When the hospital administrator's answer rambled beyond her name to detail her gener-osity, Hammett couldn't help laughing, not only at the whitewashed characterization of a woman he knew as avaricious, but also at fate for being even more contrived than the pulps, offering this absurd elev-enth-hour turn in the very hospital where he'd recently received his existential walking papers. When a nurse wheeled him from the office back to the hospital lobby, Lily greeted him with a kiss on his forehead and remarked that his color looked better, his cheeks almost rosy. He let her believe his improved color had to do with the medical treat-ment and not his unexpected discovery. Later, he visited the offices of the *New York World* and *New York Times*, where his tarnished celeb-rity still afforded him access to their file morgues, to learn more about this Brigid Paxton. Famous authors (even "blocked" ones) find no shortage of assistants eager for mention in a new book's acknowledgments. Perhaps he might yet repay in just such a fashion those who helped him, he'd thought. One last book suddenly didn't seem like too much to ask from what was left of his life. Hell, he'd dedicate it to the goddamn bird.

"How'd you find me?"

"Chance," he said.

A familiar image flashed into his mind: a sheet of watermarked paper with a stanza by Wallace Stevens typed on it. (Sometimes, Hammett typed the stanza over and over so that in the next room Lily would hear and be reassured that he was not a lost cause.)

> I know noble accents
> And lucid, inescapable rhythms;
> But I know, too,
> That the blackbird is involved
> In what I know

He glanced at the Falcon. He didn't remember setting it on the table at such an odd angle. But he must have. The damn thing couldn't have moved. The tiny black eyes were locked onto his.

He shook his head and laughed.

"What's funny?" she asked.

He thought now all that stood between him and the madhouse was for the black bird to flap its wings, bust through the window and take flight into the night. "What's funny? I'm funny," he said. "And you're funny. It's all funny when you get to the end."

"That may be, Mr. Hammett. For those who know something about their beginnings."

He took a few steps, then glanced again at the statuette—the bird's gaze had not followed him. He was not crazy, just alive. "Look, I don't know everything about your past, Mrs. Paxton."

"Nobody knows everything. Nobody needs to. Not everything. But some things . . ." She stopped, locking her eyes onto his. "Something is better than nothing."

He said nothing.

"Tell me who I am, Sam."

He looked up, straightening at the words, and took the gun from his pocket. He turned to her.

Her expression betrayed nothing.

"You called me Sam," he said, the edge in his voice palpable.

"What?"

"You called me *Sam*."

"I don't think so. Did I? Well, everyone knows your name. You're famous."

He shook his head no. "Only my oldest acquaintances call me Sam."

She looked confused. She put her hand to her head. "My head aches so," she said, tottering on the couch as if she were about to pass out.

He didn't move.

After a moment, the tottering stopped. She looked up at Hammett. Then she smiled. Her face and posture transformed. Suddenly, it was the Moira of old—before the mental institution, before the vengeful specter in the New York hotel room, seemingly vulnerable, but dangerous. "Well, you can't blame a girl for trying, eh? I had you going."

Yes she did, he thought. And if he shot her now he'd likely spare himself more trouble. "Christ, Moira. Amnesia?"

"But I had you going," she repeated.

He tapped the gun against his thigh, at once relieved and disturbed to be in the presence of the real Moira, a woman he'd have loved quite seriously if only she had been 15 percent less sociopathic. "What the hell was your scam? Where were you going with it?"

She held up her palms as if she didn't know.

"And the scar?" he asked.

She stood up off the sofa, her walk to the window displaying the old, impossible-to-ignore sashay. "A few years back, my husband accidentally hit me with his tennis racket playing doubles. Thirteen stitches." She turned back with a wry smile. "He bought me a diamond broach to make it up to me."

"You're quite the storyteller."

"Oh, you've no idea," she answered. "But soon enough you'll know."

He took a deep breath, relieved to be spared the moral confusion of a moment before. This incarnation of Moira was surely more dangerous than he'd imagined the amnesiac, Mrs. Paxton, to have been. She'd seemed an unwitting victim, momentarily confusing his priorities. Now, with the real Moira, he knew he'd have to take greater care. Nonetheless, he thought it easier to be dealing with the devil he knew.

"You betrayed me, Sam."

He didn't see an angle to going through the whole San Francisco affair again. "That's ancient history."

"There's no such thing," she snapped. "*Ancient* my ass. Everything that's ever happened might just as well have happened yesterday, might just as well be happening right now."

That seemed to him no way to live—still, he wondered if there was really any other.

"But I might forgive you yet, Sam. Do want to come upstairs? Want to stay the night with me?"

"I'm not a healthy man."

"Possessing the statuette won't help you with that."

"It's not my health that most interests me."

"Actually, the statuette won't help you with *anything*."

He gestured about the luxurious house. "It seems to have worked well enough for you."

She laughed. "The bird had nothing to do with this. This is all about me. *My* cleverness. *My* imagination. *My* ass. Do I have to spell it out for you? Is that what you need from me?"

He picked up the statuette. "Now that I have this, I need nothing from you, Moira."

She continued as if he'd said nothing. "Imagine, dear Sam, a woman clever enough to gain revenge on a lover who heartlessly sent her up the river for eleven miserable years. And how does she do this? By shooting him? Too banal. And the suffering too brief. No, she does better by spinning a yarn that strips him, a professional storyteller, of his *own ability to spin a yarn*. Could there be anything more delightfully perverse?"

"Please, Moira. No more bullshit. I'll just go now."

She moved to a spot blocking the exit to the room.

He could push past her, but he didn't want to get too close.

"Imagine that to lend credence to the story this clever woman conspires with some of the two-timing private dick's old acquaintances," she continued, beaming. "Naturally, Emil Madrid was only too happy to fill your head with the rubbish I culled from a copy of the Encyclopedia Britannica during my stay in the psych ward. The ancient Arabian angle. Remember, Sam? Of course you do. And Mike, your old partner, he covered the Norse angle, drawn from similar sources. I guess I don't have to tell you that he was only too happy to play a part in my little melodrama. And your pretty little drug-addicted secretary, who, I must admit, almost changed her mind about this when she was in your hallowed company . . . or so she told me afterwards. Nonetheless, just as you were ditching her she managed, as hired, to throw in that bit about an 'unnamed' man who was pursuing the bird with an Oriental angle."

"Hired? By you?"

"Your Lillian's not the only woman with an imagination, Sam. A magical stone, hah! Imagine a woman clever enough to conceive of such a story and resourceful enough to keep it alive for decades not on some stage or between the covers of a book but in *your* head. And then tell me that such a woman would require anything as gross as a 'lucky' statuette to gain the wealth you see around you! A woman with such an imagination would be capable of *anything*, even of finding satisfaction for a betrayal."

Hammett's head hurt. He set the statuette on a table, his throat tightening, his ears ringing.

"You don't look so good, Sam."

He gathered himself, unwilling to entertain her further with any display of what he felt. Not even anger (for fear it might transform into discernible despair). And he didn't want to shoot her because he didn't want to do the time. He took a breath and attempted to sound calm and analytical when he asked: "What about Huston?"

"The director?" She shook her head. "I never met him."

"But he said . . ."

"Oh, most men are casually superstitious," she interrupted, her hands fluttering about her face like birds. "It's because you're all so insecure, despite appearances. Believe me, I know. It's been my job to make use of that knowledge since I was a teenager."

Actually, Huston hadn't said anything specific about the bird, Hammett reflected.

"So the statuette . . . ," he started. He'd be damned if he'd finish the sentence.

She nodded, smug.

He said nothing.

"Ironically, I'd never have pulled it off if I hadn't learned how to do so from you, Sam."

He could barely speak. "What are you talking about?"

"In the psychiatric ward they only let us read kids' magazines, afraid that if we saw even a single issue of *Redbook* or the *Saturday Evening Post* we'd all return to states of raving lunacy. One such juvenile rag was called *The Young Writer's Monthly Journal*. Does that ring a bell?"

He shook his head no.

"Well, you can imagine my surprise when I discovered a 'how-to' article from 1927 written by an up-and-coming detective writer named

Dashiell Hammett. Yes, my old flame! My betrayer. You, of all people, advising kids . . . absurd! Of course, a handful of adults must have read the article too. I did anyway, over and over. And eventually I knew how to make the 'implausible' plausible."

"I remember something like that," he murmured.

"Oh, not as well as I remember. I can still quote it, Sam. Listen. 'Elements of your tale may be preposterous. What matters is not making the "fantastical" plausible to your readers; rather, what matters is that the "fantastical" seems plausible to your characters, with whom your readers identify as being true to life . . .'"

He listened.

"'And if a second character suggests support for the insupport-able,'" she continued, "'the reader will begin to reconsider what he or she thought possible in the world . . .'"

"OK Moira, enough."

But she didn't stop. "'And if a third character or element lends further credence to the story's "fantastical" elements, then the reader must accept that the story's "reality" is not bound by the limitations . . .'"

"I said stop!" Hammett snapped.

She stopped quoting. "You were my 'reader,' Sam. When you worked, all those years ago, your medium was words on a page. But mine was, well . . . myself, our old acquaintances, and you. But in the end, my technique wasn't so different than yours."

"Look, if the bird is just . . ." He stopped, sorting through it.

"If the bird's just an ordinary black stone?" she offered.

"Yeah."

"You're wondering why you wasted your life worrying about a damn rock?"

He tried to keep his expression blank, as he set the statuette on a side table.

She grinned. "Don't strain yourself, Sam. It's not rocket science. You egoists are all made of glass. For each, it's just a matter of finding the right little hammer. Usually, it's to be found in those intimate, self-pitying stories your sort tells in bed after your passion has been satisfied. When, in a woman's arms, you allow yourself for one moment to be vulnerable. In your case a fourteen-year-old dropout, an uneducated gumshoe, a second-rater. Remember? And then a little tap of the hammer into your crystalline genius and you crack. Shatter! So hopelessly suggestible. That's all any woman ever needs to know about a man to own him. Or, at least, to destroy him."

He could kill her and then kill himself, he thought. He was dying anyway, so what was losing a few months?

"Still, I'm sorry you're dying, Sam."

He looked at her, surprised. "How'd you know about that? Nobody knows. I'm not even supposed to know."

"I know everything about you. Of course, in recent years there hasn't been much new to learn."

"I don't want your sympathy."

"You think 'sympathy' has anything to do with this?"

"No."

She moved across the room and picked up the statuette, then returned it to its place on the shelf.

Hammett watched.

She turned and smiled, like a TV hostess. "I'm glad you stumbled across me, Sam. It would never have done for a man like you to die believing in silly superstitions. Even if you *lived* believing in them."

He said nothing.

She stepped toward him. "Don't take it too hard. When you get right down to it, most men don't believe in themselves. Especially big men like you."

"What makes you think I won't shoot you dead, here and now?"

She remained calm. "You're not a murderer."

"You have no idea who I am, Moira."

"Ah, but I do and I know you live by a 'code,' Sam. Remember? I know better than most. After all, you handed me over to the cops back in San Francisco because it was the 'right' thing to do."

He didn't want to go over that again. It would always come out the same. "Why the amnesia angle, Moira?"

She looked away. "Call it an inspired improvisation in a moment of weakness."

"What the hell does that mean?"

"I was caught off guard," she said, turning to him.

"Finding an armed man in your entry way?"

"No, I've always been able to handle that sort of thing. Men with guns . . ." She shook her head disdainfully. "Besides, I've always known you might eventually track me down."

He waited.

She crossed to the window, looking into the glass.

Hammett wondered if she saw something outside in the darkness, or if she was watching him in reflection. His difficulties with her had always arisen from his inability to know where her attention was truly focused at any given moment. This made her both fascinating and frustrating. And dangerous.

She spoke without turning around.

"I was caught off guard, Sam, to discover when I saw you standing there that I still loved you. Still want you. Even after all these years." She turned back to him, her eyes glistening. "Even with you looking as you do, like death warmed over. Even after I'd proven you a chump! And so, in that moment, it occurred to me that I might make you believe I'd benefited from possessing the statuette by becoming . . ." She stopped. As she struggled to find the right word, she extended her arms to her sides and opened her palms toward him, as if exposing some deep aspect of herself. "By becoming . . . a new person. Ridiculous, I know. But I thought if you saw me in a new light you might want to spend your last days with me. Call me sentimental."

He didn't know what to believe.

"You once said that 'all we've got is the fact that maybe you love me and maybe I love you,'" she continued.

"I never said that. That's a line of dialogue from the book."

"But it was what you were thinking, Sam."

"Maybe it was, maybe it wasn't. I can't say anymore."

"Well, it was like that for *me*." What was her angle now? "No angle," she said, as if once more she'd read his mind. "This whole thing has been about love, Sam."

"That's ridiculous," he snapped.

"Of course it is. Only the grift makes *sense*. Greed, avarice, lies . . . all those things are rational. But love? Jesus Christ, what else but 'ridiculous' would you expect it to be?"

He looked at her. Goddamn if she didn't seem to mean it. Had the last decades of her life been wasted, too?

"You don't believe a bad woman can love somebody?" she asked.

"I don't know the first thing about that stuff."

"Well, now you do."

He sat on the sofa. It had been a long day and an even longer night. "Bring me a drink, Moira."

She nodded and left the room.

By the time she got back, he'd had a thought—Moira, Evie, Mike, Madrid . . .

She handed him a highball and sat in a chair.

He drank and leaned towards her. "What about the Big Man?"

"Gaspereaux?"

"Yeah."

She shrugged. "What about him?"

"You got him to go along with you too?"

She laughed. "Gaspereaux died in '22, Sam. Are you losing your wits? You saw him shot down in the street."

He said nothing.

She looked at him askance. "Are you trying to trick me, Sam?"

He stood, wondering if this potboiler might yet have one more turn in it.

"What is it?" she pressed.

"Gaspereaux survived," he said.

She shook her head no. "They buried him."

"That was an imposter."

She shrugged. "OK, maybe he survived. But what does that have to do with any of this?"

"So you never saw him?"

She hesitated, working it through as best she could. "Obviously not," she answered, at last.

"Wrong answer."

She sighed. "Sam, don't do this to me, don't do it to yourself, don't do it to us."

"I'm working it through, Moira."

She spoke softly, lovingly. "That's only ever gotten you into trouble, dear."

Hammett ignored her. He crossed the room to the shelf, taking the bird once more in his hands. He considered: since Moira had not employed Gaspereaux in her scheme, where had *he* gotten the idea of the statuette's mystical powers? The chip in the stone meant nothing, either way. But since Moira never knew Gaspereaux survived the shooting, she couldn't have told him about any Egyptian angle. Therefore, he must have come upon the mystical anecdote through some other source, perhaps a reliable one.

Hammett looked at the statuette.

It was heavy and hard in his hands. But it was also warm, almost as if it were a living thing.

Then he looked at Moira, the best he'd ever known.

She ran her hand through her auburn hair. "Sam, what trick is your mind playing on you?"

He'd learned long before never to trust a woman who told him not to think things through.

"Sam?" she pressed.

Was it possible she'd actually employed Evie, Mike, and Madrid not just to torment him with stories of the bird's mystical powers, but also to provide a plausible cover story should he ever catch wind of the same stories through another source, track her down, and come after the treasure, as he had tonight? Might she have instructed their old acquaintances to tell him the *truth* (unbeknownst to them), so that if she was ever pressed by Hammett she could point to their "vengefully motivated" employment as evidence they'd duped him, suggestive that the mystical nature of the statuette was, regardless of whatever he might have heard elsewhere, nothing more than a wronged woman's outrageous lie? How better to disguise a macabre truth than as an all-too-human subversion? A reversal of a reversal—telling the truth to deceive. So, might the power of the statuette be real after all? he mused. Ordinarily, he'd have dismissed such convolutions as mere paranoia. But when it came to Moira's capacity to deceive, paranoia seemed an asset.

"Sam?" she repeated. "What's wrong?"

And mightn't her amnesia story have been just an initial attempt to persuade him to leave the premises without the bird, banking on his reluctance to steal from an "innocent" woman, the philanthropist Mrs. Brigid Paxton, amnesiac? Sure, once exposed, Moira had admitted to the lie, but she'd characterized it as an effort to win him back. What kind of sap would believe that? Nonetheless, her improvisations were imaginative, unpredictable, and well-grounded in character. He recognized in them something of his own lost creative energy. Well, she'd had the damn bird. And now, he realized that his sudden, elaborate postulations about what may or may not have happened were not dissimilar to the conceptualizing of labyrinthine plot twists that used to fuel and fire his writing years before. He looked again at the statuette in his hands. Was all this just wishful thinking? (In the end, is there any other kind?) Or was he suddenly not just a detective, a dreamer, or a paranoid, but a writer again?

She stood and started toward him.

He held his palm up to stop her.

There was an alternative, he thought. Maybe she *had* loved him all these years, as she claimed. Maybe she *had* expressed her pain through a brilliant and perverse revenge, robbing him of that which he valued most by clouding his imagination with self-doubt. Maybe the statuette was truly nothing more than a weathered eyesore. But what then of Cletus Gaspereaux? Hammett ran through the possibilities. Might the Big Man simply have been the ripe victim of some other grifter's con based on a rumor of a mystical statuette—a rumor coincidentally generated by Evie, Mike, and Madrid's lies about the damned thing? After all, tall tales spread like social diseases among the criminal set.

The truth was a pendulum, swinging back and forth.

Finally, there was no way to know, short of asking Moira to be truthful. And that was no option.

"I don't know what's real anymore," he said.

She nodded sympathetically and went to him. He didn't stop her. Scented of lilac, she put one hand gently to his gaunt, weathered face. Her satiny skin felt good. She turned his chin to her and kissed him softly on the lips. Meantime, with her other hand she expertly slipped the .38 from his jacket pocket and then stepped away.

He observed her doing all of it.

"This gun is real," she said.

"Don't count on it, Moira."

"So what are you going to do, my Sam Hammett?"

He said nothing.

"Are you going to leave with the bird?" she pressed. "Or leave without the bird? Or not leave at all?"

In answer, with statuette in hand, he started out of the room.

"Stop!" she snapped.

He didn't stop.

"Fine, then go," she shouted. "Just go! Wait. Stop!"

He took two more steps before he heard the metallic click of the gun's firing pin behind him.

He turned.

She had already dropped the .38 to the rug.

With his free hand, he reached into his other jacket pocket and removed the six bullets, rattling them in his palm before tossing them into far corners of the room.

A tear streamed down her cheek. She fell to her knees. "The gun wasn't aimed at you, Sam." She pointed with her index finger at her own temple and squeezed off an imaginary shot with her thumb. "Believe me."

Outside, it had begun to snow.

Crossing the hushed yard to his car, Hammett held the Falcon statuette inside his wool coat to protect it from the elements.

THE END

AFTERWORD

BY GORDON McALPINE

I discovered the heretofore unknown, typed copy of the preceding manuscript, *Hammett Unwritten* by Owen Fitzstephen, in the spring of 2012 at the bottom of a cardboard box in the Lillian Hellman collection of the Harry Ransom Center at the University of Texas, Austin. As I was then engaged in research for a doctoral dissertation about Hellman's dialectical use of anatomical imagery, I initially paid little attention to the dusty manuscript, assuming it was merely the apprentice work of one or another of Hellman's acquaintances who'd likely hoped to gain her critique. After all, there was no mention of the title or author anywhere in Hellman's papers and no record of either on the Library of Congress web site. Nonetheless, I awoke a few nights later at 3 a.m., agitated by the sudden realization that I recognized the name of the author, Owen Fitzstephen, from some place. Climbing out of bed, I performed a Google search that immediately suggested literary possibilities so rich that in their subsequent pursuit I would not only abandon my dissertation, but, ultimately, my home and identity.

Owen Fitzstephan is the name of a character in Dashiell Hammett's second novel, *The Dain Curse* (1929). In that book, Hammett described Fitzstephan, a successful writer of mystery stories, in a manner that is difficult to read as anything but autobiographical. "[A] long, lean . . . man with sleepy gray eyes . . . who pretended to be lazier than he was, would rather talk than do anything else, and had a lot of what seemed to be accurate information and original ideas on any subject that happened to come up, as long as it was a little out of the ordinary." The implications of such an autobiographical identification are enriched by the fact that Fitzstephan is ultimately revealed to be the novel's evil mastermind. (Indeed, when his duplicitous plot is uncovered, shortly after he has suffered the loss of one arm, one leg, and half his face in an explosion, he is carted off to a hospital for the criminally insane.) Over the years, numerous academic papers have examined the psychological, literary, and political aspects of Hammett's rich choice of doppelganger in *The Dain Curse*. But what immediately fascinated me was the question of why the name of a fictional character would be cited as the author of an unpublished, book-length manuscript found in a dusty box among Lillian Hellman's collected papers. And I couldn't help but wonder if the slight variation in spelling (Fitzstephan versus Fitzstephen) had been intended as a signal to the reader to devot particular attention to the question of authorship.

After reading the manuscript, I felt certain that only one man could have written it. Ironically, it is the one man for whom the nom de plume is least concealing—Hammett himself. At that point, I ceased work on my doctoral dissertation. Poring through a handful of Hammett biographies, I discovered nothing factual to contradict the possibility that I had indeed stumbled across Hammett's final book, presumably written between January 1, 1960, and his death from lung cancer on January 10, 1961.

Of course, questions arise.

For example, is the preceding manuscript Hammett's final novel, featuring an uncharacteristically postmodern use of his own name and persona as the protagonist, or is it a chronologically wide-ranging but thematically tightly focused memoir that utilizes fictional techniques for dramatic effect? After researching numerous period materials, I am convinced it is the latter. First, consider the Hammett-character's resolution in the final chapter to dedicate an as-yet unwritten book to "the bird," and then glance back to the actual dedication page of this manuscript. And that is just the start. The details of the Black Falcon case from San Francisco, 1922, are a matter of record, as exemplified by the yellowed newspaper article I discovered paper clipped to the first page of the manuscript (published here on page 9). Numerous other sources can still easily be obtained. For example, records indicate that Hammett's former secretary Evie LeFabre indeed died of a drug overdose, 1939; Hammett's former partner Mike Arnette died in a train wreck in Pennsylvania, 1954; Emil Madrid died of a heart attack in federal prison, 1957; Moira O'Shea was released from a California hospital for the criminally insane in 1933 and thereafter appears in no further government documents. However, it would seem that her death attracted the most attention of the four. Every New York newspaper covered the story of an auburn-haired, sixty-four-year-old philanthropist named Mary Price, wealthy widow of a university president, who committed suicide in her Long Island home with an unregistered .38 caliber handgun around midnight on New Year's Eve, 1959. Mrs. Price left no suicide note. Although police found indications that at some time that evening she entertained an unidentified visitor, further investigation unearthed no evidence of homicide. Interestingly, Mrs. Price's was thereby the only name Hammett saw fit to change in his manuscript. Whether this was a gesture of respect, disdain, or something else altogether, we will never know. As for any differences in prose style that critics may perceive between the preceding manuscript and Hammett's earlier known work, I suggest that the roughly three decades that separate his periods of literary productivity are explanation enough.

Another question is why the typed manuscript would have been among Lillian Hellman's papers and yet never have received from her the sort of attention (including publication) it would seem to have demanded. A clue to this mystery may be found in Hellman's introduction to an anthology of Hammett's novels, published a few years after his death. "I have been asked many times over the years why he did not write another novel after *The Thin Man*," she writes. "I do not know . . . he kept his work, and his plans for work, in angry privacy and even I would not have been answered if I had ever asked, and maybe because I never asked is why I was with him until the last day of his life." I believe this is pure deceit. (Hellman was not known for accuracy when reporting details of her life.) Judging from the alternative account in *Hammett Unwritten*, it seems Hammett often spoke with Hellman about his writer's block and in so doing seems to have embarrassed her with his increasingly nagging suspicions that his troubles had to do with the statuette known as the Black Falcon. Is it possible that when Hellman discovered the completed manuscript in the last days of Hammett's life she chose to shelve it to spare him what she feared would be embarrassing revelations, or, alternatively, to spare herself being outshone by another woman, Moira O'Shea, and thereby being dethroned in the public's eye as the most powerful and interesting woman in Dashiell Hammett's life? These reservations also serve to discount the theory put forth by some of my colleagues that Lillian Hellman may have penned the manuscript. Yes, the book is structured and paced almost as much like an evening in the theatre (discreet scenes, interior locations, extended dialogues) as it is a novel; however, I believe Hammett's deepening interest and exposure to the stage during his decades' long relationship with one of America's top playwrights serves as more than sufficient explanation for whatever "theatrical"-seeming choices may characterize the work.

Finally, there is the question of why I, too, have chosen a pen name, even for this insignificant afterword. Gordon McAlpine is the name of a professor in California who once told me in an undergraduate class (grade: C–) that my inability to write even two pages for a creative writing assignment need not be regarded as a complete failure but rather as affirmation that I may yet find my true vocation as a literary critic, unearthing truths buried in *other people's fictions*. He could not have been more correct, doubtless saving me years of fruitlessness. His prescience is all the more impressive because he could not have known that one day I would literally unearth *Hammett Unwritten* from its dusty tomb. And, truthfully, the manuscript is not all I unearthed that day. The other neglected item I found in the cardboard box in the Lillian Hellman collection was a primitive black statuette in the shape of a falcon. I took it and have kept it, much to my advantage. This, of course, is why I have no choice but to use a pseudonym. Though I am not worried about either the Austin or University of Texas police departments tracking me down (I've moved far, far away), I cannot claim that I don't suffer occasional sleepless nights, wondering if there remain any descendants from Hammett's old set who might yet lust after the bird.

ENDNOTES

1. The description of Brigid O'Shaughnessy in *The Maltese Falcon* actually reads "erect and high breasted."

2. The March 30, 1922, edition of the *San Francisco Examiner* identifies the location of Gaspereaux's memorial service as the Blaisedale & Sons Funeral Parlor on Market Street.

3. In *The Maltese Falcon*, Hammett describes the Fat Man's daughter, Rhea, as "a brown-eyed, fair-haired smallish girl of seventeen whom the hotel-staff said was beautiful."

4. In *The Maltese Falcon*, Hammett describes the attire of Madrid's counterpart, Joel Cairo, as follows: "A square-cut ruby, its sides paralleled by four baguette diamonds gleamed against the deep green of his cravat ... The uppers of his patent-leather shoes were hidden by fawn spats. He held a black derby hat in a chamois-gloved hand ..."

5. In an unpublished memoir, restaurateur Alfredo Sardi Jr. recalled with regret that Hammett's caricature was actually removed in response to a "powerfully expressed request" from federal authorities at the time of Hammett's criminal prosecution.

ACKNOWLEDGMENTS

My warmest thanks to those whose advice helped me unearth the black bird: Mark Iger, Roy Langsdon, Mark Rosen, Richard Smith, and Robert Ward. Additionally, I am grateful to Phillip Spitzer and Lukas Ortiz, who handled the project with care and expertise, and to Dan Mayer for his courage in embarking on the bold venture that is Seventh Street Books. Finally, I'd never have found my way through all the twists and turns without the daily inspiration of my own band of fugitives—Jonathan, Shane, Harlan, and my beloved and steadfast partner-in-crime, Julie.

❖

—G. M.

ABOUT THE AUTHORS

Owen Fitzstephen is an accomplished practitioner of what Dashiell Hammett called "the literary grift."

Gordon McAlpine is the author of numerous novels as well as a middle-grade trilogy, The Misadventures of Edgar and Allan Poe. Additionally, he is coauthor of the nonfiction book *The Way of Baseball: Finding Stillness at 95 MPH*. He has taught creative writing and literature at UC Irvine, UCLA, and Chapman University. He lives with his wife, Julie, in Southern California.